"When you have finished your coffee, perhaps you would like to dance?" Blaize suggested. "After all, we are supposed to be lovers, despite that virginal look of yours...."

Petra's mouth compressed and she put down her coffee cup with a small clatter. "That's it!" she told him forcefully. "From now on, every time you so much as mention my...my...the word *virgin*, I shall deduct five dollars from your fee! I am paying you to help me escape a marriage I don't want, not to keep on bringing up something that has nothing whatsoever to do with our business arrangement!"

"No? I beg to differ," Blaize informed her softly. "I am supposed to create the impression that I am seducing you," he reminded her. "Who is going to believe that if you insist on looking like a..."

"Five dollars!" Petra warned him.

"Like a woman who does not know what it is to experience a man's passion," Blaize finished silkily.

Penny Jordan

THE SHEIKH'S VIRGIN BRIDE

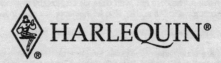

Arabian Nights

HARLEQUIN®

TORONTO • NEW YORK • LONDON
AMSTERDAM • PARIS • SYDNEY • HAMBURG
STOCKHOLM • ATHENS • TOKYO • MILAN • MADRID
PRAGUE • WARSAW • BUDAPEST • AUCKLAND

ISBN 0-373-12325-6

THE SHEIKH'S VIRGIN BRIDE

First North American Publication 2003.

Copyright © 2003 by Penny Jordan.

Printed in U.S.A.

CHAPTER ONE

'DID you check out the sexy windsurfer attendant like I told you?'

'Yeah! He was everything you said and more—much, much more. He's coming up to my room later. Mind you, he did say that he'd have to be careful. Apparently he's already on a warning from this Sheikh Rashid—the guy who co-owns the hotel—for fraternising with guests.'

'And you did more than just "fraternise", right?'

'Yeah, much, much more.'

From her seat under the protective sun umbrella of the rooftop bar of the Marina Restaurant where she had just finished lunch, the conversation of the two women standing next to her chair was plainly audible to Petra. Still discussing the sexual attributes of the Zuran resort complex's windsurfing instructor, they started to move away. Realising that one of them had dropped her wrap, Petra picked it up, interrupting their discussion to return it and earning herself a brief thank you from its owner.

As they walked away, still engrossed in their conversation, Petra grinned appreciatively to herself, murmuring wholeheartedly beneath her breath, 'Thank *you*!'

Although they didn't realise it, thanks to them she had just been given access to the very thing she had been looking for for the last two days!

As soon as they were out of sight she got up, collecting her own wrap, although unlike them she had chosen to eat her lunch wearing a silky pair of wide-legged casual trousers over her tankini top, instead of merely her swimwear.

Shading her eyes from the glare of the sun, she summoned the waiter who had served her her meal.

'Excuse me,' she asked him, 'can you tell me where the windsurfers are?'

Half an hour later Petra was lying on a sun lounger, carefully positioned by the attentive beach attendant who had asked her where she wanted to sit so that she had a direct and uninterrupted view of the stunning man-made bay which was home to the resort's pleasure craft, and an equally direct and uninterrupted view of the windsurfing instructor she had overheard discussed so enthusiastically over lunch!

She could certainly appreciate just why her fellow guests had waxed so lyrical about him!

Petra was used to seeing good-looking muscular men; she had attended an American university and, since the death of her parents in an accident when she was seventeen, she had travelled extensively both in Europe and Australia with her godfather, the senior British diplomat who had been her parents' closest friend. She'd become, therefore, quite familiar with the sexy beach bum super-stud macho type of man who thought he was heaven's gift to the female sex.

And this man certainly filled all the physical specifications for the type! And then some!

He could easily earn a living modelling designer underwear, Petra acknowledged as her own rush of sensual heat caught her discomfortingly off guard.

But as she watched him Petra was unwillingly forced to admit he had something else; something extra.

He was gathering up some discarded boards, and even the regulation smart hotel shorts had the effect of heightening his sexuality rather than discreetly concealing it.

Across the distance that separated them Petra could some-how sense his maleness, and almost feel the testosterone-laden aura that surrounded him. The movement of his body as he worked reminded Petra of the coiled suppleness of a hunting panther—every movement, every breath a perfect harmony of honed strength and focus, not one single jot of energy wasted or superfluous.

She could see the way the sunlight highlighted the mus-cle structure of his arm as he held the windsurfer, the breeze tousling the thick darkness of his hair. From beneath their designer sunglasses she suspected that every woman on the beach must be watching him, and perhaps holding their breath as they did so, as she herself was doing. He had a mesmerising presence about him that was wholly and shockingly sexual, a rawness that Petra acknowledged was compelling, challenging, and very, very dangerously excit-ing! Oh, yes! He was exactly what she needed! The more she watched him, the more she was sure of it!

Compulsively she watched him from the safety of the distance that separated them.

Over an hour later, on her way back to her luxurious hotel suite, Petra was busily making plans. As she crossed the busy *souq* area of the complex, Petra paused to watch in admiration as a craftsman skilfully hammered a piece of metal into shape.

It was no wonder that this particular complex had re-ceived such worldwide acclaim. From the seductive appeal of its Moorish design, with its fragrant enclosed gardens, to its palatial extravaganza of expensive boutiques and the traditional flavour of its recreated *souq*, the complex breathed magic and romance and most of all wealth.

Petra still could not get her head round the fact that in all there were over twenty different restaurants situated around the complex, serving food from virtually every part of the world, but right now food was the last thing on her mind.

From her hotel bedroom Petra could just about see the beach. The sexy macho windsurfer had disappeared midway through the afternoon, climbing aboard one of the gleaming and very obviously fast boats moored at the adjoining marina, and Petra's last sight of him had been of the sunshine gleaming on the thick darkness of his hair and the golden bronze of his tanned skin.

He was back now, though, even though the beach itself was deserted as the sun started to dip towards the horizon. Methodically he was collecting the abandoned windsurfers, and the other small pleasure craft the complex made available to its guests.

This was the perfect opportunity for her to do what she had been wanting to do ever since she had overheard the two women discussing him!

Before her courage could desert her she picked up her jacket and headed for her suite door.

Down on the beach it was almost dusk, the cool chill in the air reminding Petra that, despite the fact that the daytime temperature was in the high twenties, in this part of the world it was still winter.

For a second she thought she was too late, that the beach bum had gone, and her heart plummeted sharply with disappointment—her gaze searching the darkening beach.

As she stood looking out across the pretty marina Petra was so lost in her own thoughts that the sudden darkness of a shadow thrown across the fading light shocked her.

Spinning round, she sucked in her stomach on a shocked breath as she realised that the object of her thoughts was

standing in front of her, and so close to her that a single
step forward would bring them body to body.

Instinctively Petra wanted to step back, but the stubborn
pride that her father had once insisted she had inherited
directly from her grandfather refused to let her move.

Lifting her head, she took a deep breath, then exhaled it
unsteadily as she realised that she had not lifted her head
enough, and that right now instead of making contact with
his eyes her gaze was resting helplessly on the curve of his
mouth.

What was it they said about men with a full bottom lip?
That they were very sensual, very tactile…men who knew
all the secret nuances of pleasures the touch of those male
lips could have on a woman?

Petra felt faintly dizzy. She hadn't realised he was so
tall. What nationality was he? Italian? Greek? His hair was
very dark and very thick, and his skin—as she had had
every opportunity to observe earlier in the day—was a
deep, warm golden brown. He was fully dressed now, in a
white tee shirt, jeans and trainers, and somehow—despite
his casual clothes—he was disconcertingly much more for-
midable and authoritative-looking than she had expected.

It was almost fully dark; tiny decorative lights were
springing up all around them, illuminating the marina and
its environs. Petra could see the searing flash of his eyes
as his glance encompassed her. First almost dismissively,
and then appraisingly, his body stiffening as though suddenly alerted to something about her that had caught his
interest, awakened his hunting instinct, changing the uninterest she could have sworn she had initially seen in his
eyes to a narrowed intense concentration that pinned her
into wary immobility.

If she turned and ran now he would enjoy it—enjoy pursuing her, tormenting her, she decided nervily. He was that kind of man!

Despite the fact that she was wearing a perfectly respectable pair of jeans and a shirt, she suddenly felt as though he could see right through them to the flesh beneath her clothes, that already he knew every curve of her, every hidden secret and vulnerability. She was not used to experiencing such feelings and they threw her a little off guard.

'If you've come looking for one-to-one lessons, I'm afraid you've left it too late.'

The open cynicism in his voice was something she had not been prepared for, and both it and the look he was giving her burned her skin. Petra suspected she could hear a hundred generations of male contempt for a certain type of female wantonness.

'Actually, I don't need lessons,' she told him, immediately rallying her pride. She had learned to windsurf as a young teenager, and although he wasn't to know it she'd reached competition standard.

'No? Then what do you need?' his soft insultingly knowing response shocked through her.

Petra could understand how those women had been so excited by him! He possessed a sexual aura, a sexual magnetism that dizzied her senses. His air of control and self-assurance hinted tauntingly at the fact that he considered he had the power to overwhelm and dominate her if he chose to do so, that he knew precisely the effect he had on her sex! This was a man whose very existence spelled a very distinct kind of predatory male dangerousness in any language. Which was exactly why he was so perfect for what she wanted, she reminded herself as she tussled with an unfamiliar and ignominious urge to turn and run whilst she still had the option to do so.

Irritated by her own weakness, she refused to give in to it. In her time she had faced down a wide array of men for a wide variety of reasons, and there was no way she was going to be out-faced by this one! Even if it was the first time she had ever been made so overwhelmingly aware of a man's sexuality that she could barely breathe the air that surrounded them because it was so charged with raw rogue testosterone.

Ignoring what she was feeling, Petra took a deep breath and told him firmly, 'I have a proposition to put to you.'

In the silence that followed her statement he must have moved slightly, she recognised, because suddenly she could see his full face—and what she could see made the breath seize in her lungs. She had known this afternoon that he had the kind of powerful male allure that could neither be imitated nor acquired, but now she realised that he also had the kind of facial features that would have made a Greek god weep with envy.

The only thing she couldn't see was the colour of his eyes. But surely with such colouring they had to be brown. Brown! Inwardly Petra allowed herself to relax a little. Brown-eyed men had never appealed to her. Secretly she had always hankered for a man with the cool magnetism of pure silver-grey-coloured eyes, having fallen in love with the hero of a book she had read as a young teenager whose eyes had been that colour.

'A proposition?' The cynical uninterest in his voice made her face burn a little. 'I'm a man,' he told her bluntly. 'And I don't go to bed with women who proposition me. I like to hunt my own prey, not be hunted by it. Of course if you're really desperate I could give you directions to a place where you might have more luck.'

As she felt her fingers curling into small, angry fists, Petra had to resist the instinctive temptation to react to his insult in the most basic female way possible. Satisfactory though it might initially be, slapping his face was hardly going to be conducive to concluding her plan successfully, she reminded herself wryly. At least his attitude confirmed her assumption that he was a sexual predator—not the kind of man a potential husband would want consorting with the woman he wanted to make his wife. In short this man was ideal for her purpose.

'It isn't that kind of proposition,' she denied firmly.

'No...? So what kind is it, then?' he challenged her.

'The kind that pays well and isn't illegal,' Petra replied promptly, crossing her fingers and hoping inwardly that her comment would have piqued his interest.

He had moved again, and now Petra realised that it was her turn to have her features revealed to him in the increasing illumination of the decorative lights.

She wasn't a vain person, but she knew that she was generally considered to be attractive. But if this man found her so, he certainly wasn't showing it, she acknowledged as she was subjected to a cool visual inspection that made her itch to step back into the protective shadows, her arms wrapped protectively around her body.

'Sounds fascinating,' he mocked her laconically. 'What do I have to do?'

Petra allowed herself to begin to relax. 'Pursue me and seduce me—very publicly,' she told him.

Just for a second she had the satisfaction of seeing that she had surprised him. His eyes widened fractionally before he controlled the movement.

'Seduce you?' he repeated. And now it was Petra's turn to be surprised, and unpleasantly so, as she marked the sharp curtness in a male voice that had abruptly become disconcertingly chilly.

'Not for real,' she told him quickly, before he could say

anything more. 'What I want is for you to pretend to seduce me.'

'Pretend? Why?' he demanded baldly. 'Do you already have a lover you wish to make jealous? Is that it?' he guessed insultingly.

Petra glared at him.

'No, I do not. I want to pay you to ensure that I lose my…my reputation.'

For one unguarded moment Petra saw his face and wondered exactly what the sudden frown creasing his forehead and the complete stillness of his body meant.

'Am I allowed to ask why you want to lose it?' he asked her.

'You can ask,' Petra told him. 'But I don't intend to tell you.'

'No? Well, in that case, I don't intend to help you.'

He was already turning away from her and Petra started to panic.

'I'm prepared to pay you five thousand pounds,' she called out to him.

'Ten thousand and then we might…just might have a deal,' he told her softly as he stopped and turned to look at her.

Ten thousand pounds. Petra felt sick. Her parents had left her a very generous trust fund, but until she turned twenty-five, there was no way she could raise such a large sum without the approval of her trustees—one of whom was her godfather, who was after all part of the reason why she needed to do this in the first place.

Her body slumped in defeat.

He was still walking away from her, and had almost reached the end of the beach. In another few seconds he would be gone.

Swallowing against the bitter taste of her own failure, she turned away herself.

CHAPTER TWO

REFUSING to give in to the temptation of watching him disappear, Petra fixed her gaze on the sea.

Most people, on first seeing her, assumed that Petra carried either Spanish or Italian blood in her veins. Her skin had a soft creamy warmth and her dark brown hair was thick and lustrous, her bone structure elegant and delicately patrician. Only her brilliant green eyes and the narrow straightness of her small nose, combined with her passionate nature, gave away the fact that she possessed Celtic genes, inherited through her American father's Irish ancestry. Very few people guessed that her colouring came from an exotic blending of those genes with her mother's Bedouin blood.

She could feel the evening breeze lifting her hair, its coolness raising tiny goosebumps on her skin, but they were nothing to the rash of sensation that flooded atavistically through her body as she suddenly felt the pressure of a male hand on the nape of her neck.

'Five thousand, then—and the reason,' a now familiar silken voice whispered in her ear.

He had come back! Petra didn't know whether to be elated or horrified!

'No haggling!' the silken voice warned her. 'Five thousand and the reason, or no deal.'

Petra's throat had gone dry. She didn't want to tell him, but what option did she have? And besides, what harm could it really do?

'Very well.'

What was it that was making her voice sound so tremulous? Surely not the fact that his hand was still on her nape?

'You're trembling,' he told her, so accurately tracking and trapping her own thoughts that his intuitiveness shocked her. 'Why? Are you afraid? Excited?'

As he drawled the soft words with deliberate slowness, almost whispering into her ear, his thumb stroked against the side of her throat, trapping the pulse fluttering there.

Stalwartly Petra wrenched herself free and told him resolutely. 'Neither! I'm just cold.'

She could see the taunting cruelty in the mocking curve of his smile.

'Of course,' he agreed. 'So, you want me to publicly pursue and seduce you?'

He questioned her as though he had suddenly grown bored with tormenting her, like a domestic cat suddenly tiring of the prey it had caught as a plaything rather than for food. But this man was no domesticated fireside pet! No, everything he did had a raw, untamed danger about it, a warning of power mockingly leashed.

'Why? Tell me!'

Petra took a deep breath.

'It's a long and complicated story,' she warned him.

'Tell me!' he repeated.

Briefly Petra closed her eyes, trying to marshal her thoughts into logical order, and then opened them again, beginning quietly, 'My father was an American diplomat. He met my mother here in Zuran when he was posted here. They fell in love but her father did not approve. He had other plans for her. He believes that it is a daughter's duty to allow herself to be used as a pawn in her family's empire-building.' As she spoke Petra could hear the anger and the bitterness in her own voice, just as she could feel it surging inside her—a mixture of a long-standing old pain on behalf of her mother and a much newer, bitter anger for herself.

'My grandfather refused to have anything to do with my mother after she ran away with my father. And he forbade his family—my mother's brothers and their wives—from having anything to do with her either. But she told me all about him. How cruel he had been!' Petra's eyes flashed.

'My parents were wonderfully, blissfully happy, but they were killed in an accident when I was seventeen. I went to live in England with my godfather who, like my father, is a diplomat. That's how they met—when my godfather was with the British Embassy in Zuran. Everything was fine. I finished university and then I travelled with my godfather, I worked for an aid agency in the field, and I was…am planning to take my Master's. But then…

'A short time ago, my uncle came to London and made contact with my godfather. He told him that my grandfather wanted to see me. That he wanted me to come to Zuran. I didn't want to have anything to do with him. I knew how much he had hurt my mother. She never stopped hoping that he would forgive her, that he would answer her letters, accept an olive branch, but he never did. Not even when she and my father were killed. He never even acknowledged her death. No one from my family here came to the funeral. He would not allow them to do so!'

Tears of rage and pain momentarily filled Petra's eyes, but determinedly she blinked them away.

'My godfather begged me to reconsider. He said it was what my parents would have wanted—for the family to be reconciled. He told me that my grandfather was one of the major shareholders in this holiday complex and he had suggested that both I and my godfather come and stay here, get to know one another. I wanted to refuse, but…' She stopped and shook her head. 'I felt for my mother's sake that I had to come. But if I'd known then the real reason why I was being brought out here—!'

'The real reason?' There was a brusqueness in the male voice that rasped roughly against her sensitive emotions.

'Yes, the real reason,' she reiterated bitterly.

'The day we arrived my uncle came here to the hotel with his wife, and his son—my cousin Saud. He's only fifteen, and… They said that my grandfather wasn't well enough to come, that he had a serious heart condition, and that his doctor had said that he needed bed rest and no excitement. I believed them. But then, when we were on our own together, Saud accidentally let the cat out of the bag. He had no idea, you see, that I didn't know what was really going on!'

Petra shook her head as she heard her voice starting to tremble. 'Far from merely wanting to meet me, to put right the wrong he had done to my parents, what my grandfather actually wants is to marry me off to one of his business partners! And, unbelievably, my godfather actually thinks it's a good idea.

'Although at first he tried to pretend that I had got it wrong and misunderstood Saud, in fact my godfather thinks it's so much of a good idea that right now he's incommunicado in the far east—on official diplomatic business, of course—and he's taken my passport with him! "Just meet the chap, Petra, old thing."' She mimicked her godfather's cut-glass upper class British voice savagely. '"No harm in doing that, eh? Who knows? You might find you actually rather like him. Look at British nobility. All from arranged marriages, and with pretty good results generally speaking. All that love tosh. Doesn't always work y'know. Like to like, that's what I always say—and from what your uncle has to say—it seems like this Sheikh Rashid and you have lots in common. Similar cultural heritage. Bound to go down well with the Foreign Office. And the Prime Minister…awfully keen on that sort of thing, y'know. I've heard it on the grapevine that the White House is one hundred per cent behind the idea.'''

'Your grandfather wants you to marry a man who is a fellow countryman of his, and a business colleague, as a PR exercise for diplomatic purposes? Is that what you're telling me?' He cut across Petra's angry outburst incisively.

Petra could hear the cynical disbelief in his voice and didn't really blame him for his reaction.

'Well, my godfather would like me to think that's the only motivation for my grandfather's behaviour, but of course he isn't anything like so high-minded or altruistic,' she told him scathingly.

'From what I've managed to find out from Saud, my grandfather wants me to marry this man because as well as being a fellow shareholder in this complex he is also very well connected—is in fact related to the Zuran Royal Family, no less! My mother was originally supposed to marry a second cousin of the Family before she met and fell in love with my father. Her father—my grandfather—considered it to be a very prestigious match, and one that would bring him a lot of benefits. I suppose in his eyes it is only fitting that since he couldn't marry my mother off to suit his own ends I should now take her place as a…a victim to his greed and ambition!'

'Does your mixed heritage disturb you?' His unexpected question threw Petra a little.

'Disturb me?' She tensed, anger and pride ignited inside her. 'No! Why should it?' she challenged him. 'I am proud to be the product of my parents' love for one another, and proud to be myself as well.'

'You misunderstand me. The disturbance I refer to is that

caused by the volatile mixing of the coldness of the north with the heat of the desert; Anglo Saxon blood mixed with Bedouin, the hunger for roots and the compulsion that drives the nomad and everything that those two polar opposites encompass. Do you never feel torn, pulled in two different ways by two different cultures? A part of both of them and at the same time alien to them?'

His words so accurately summed up the feelings that had bedevilled Petra for as long as she had been able to recognise them that they stunned her into silence. How could he possibly know that she felt like that? The tiny hairs on her skin lifted as though she were in the presence of a force she could not fully understand—a strength and insight so much more developed than her own that she felt in awe of it.

'I am what I am,' she told him firmly as she fought to ignore the way he was making her feel.

'And what is that?'

Anger darkened her eyes.

'I am a modern, independent woman who will not be manipulated or used to serve the ends of a machiavellian old man.'

She could see the shrug he gave.

'If you do not want to marry the husband your grandfather has chosen for you then why do you simply not tell him so?'

'It isn't that easy,' Petra was forced to admit. 'Of course I told my godfather that there was totally and absolutely no way I was going to agree to even meet this man. Never mind marry him. That was when he announced that he had to leave for the far east and that he was taking my passport with him. To give me time to get to know my grandfather and to rediscover my cultural heritage, was how he put it, but of course I know what he's really hoping for. He's hoping that by leaving me here, at my grandfather's mercy, he will be able to pressure me into doing what he wants. My godfather retires next year, and no doubt he's hoping that the government will reward him for his work—including arranging a high-profile marriage to Sheikh Rashid—with a Peerage in the New Year's honours list. And what makes it even worse is that, from what my cousin Saud has told me, it seems the whole family believe I should be thrilled to think that this…this…man is prepared to consider marrying me,' Petra concluded bitterly.

'Like normally marries like in such circumstances,' the cool, almost bored voice pointed out. 'I understand what you are saying about your grandfather's motivations, but what about those of your proposed husband? Why should this…?'

'Sheikh Rashid,' Petra supplied for him grimly. 'The same Sheikh Rashid who, from what I hear, does not approve of your…behaviour with his female guests!'

The quick, hard look he gave her caused Petra to say immediately, 'I heard two women discussing you earlier on—' She stopped. 'As to why the Sheikh should want to marry me…' Petra took a deep breath. 'You might well ask. But apparently he and I have something in common—we are both of mixed parentage, only in his case I believe that it was his father who provided his Zuran heritage and not his mother. More importantly, The Zuran Royal Family consider the marriage to be a good idea. My godfather says that it will cause great offence if he refuses a marriage they have given their seal of approval, and great offence to mine if he refuses me. However, whilst I know enough about Zuran culture to know that for either of us to refuse the other once negotiations have commenced is considered to be an unforgivable insult, I know too that if he were to have reason to believe that morally I am not fit to be his wife he could honourably refuse to accept me.'

'There's an awful lot of supposition going on here,' came the wry comment.

But when Petra shot him a fulminatingly angry look, and demanded, 'Are you trying to say that it's all in my imagination? Then there's no point in us wasting any more of one another's time!'

He gave her a small semi-placatory look and offered conciliatingly, 'So! I understand the motivation, but why choose me?'

Petra gave a small cynical shrug.

'Like I said, I heard a couple of female guests discussing you earlier, and from what they were saying it was obvious that…'

When she stopped speaking, he prompted her softly, 'That what?'

'That you have a reputation for enjoying the favours of the women who stay here. So much so, in fact,' she added, tilting her chin defiantly, 'that you have already been reprimanded for your behaviour by…by Sheikh Rashid, and are in danger of losing your job!' Petra gave a small shudder. 'I don't know how those women can cheapen themselves! I might not want an arranged marriage, but there is no way I would ever prejudice my own personal moral beliefs by indulging in a meaningless sexual fling a…a cheap sexual thrill!' Through the darkness Petra was suddenly acutely conscious of his gaze fixing intently on her.

'I see… So you don't want an arranged marriage and you don't want cheap sexual thrills. So what do you want?'

'Nothing!' As he turned his head Petra saw the mocking way he raised his eyebrows and defended herself immediately. 'What I mean is I don't want anything until I meet a man who…'

'Who matches up to your very high standards?' he suggested tauntingly.

Crossly Petra shook her head.

'Please don't put words into my mouth. What I was going to say was until I meet a man I can love and respect and…and want to…to commit myself to emotionally, mentally, cerebrally, sexually—every which way there is. That is the kind of relationship my parents shared,' she told him passionately. 'And that is the kind of relationship I want for myself and one day want to encourage my own children to aspire to.'

'A tall order, especially in this day and age,' came the blunt response.

'Perhaps, but one I think it worth waiting to fulfil,' Petra told him firmly.

'Aren't you afraid that if you finally meet this paragon he might be deterred by the fact that your reputation—?'

'No.' Petra interrupted him swiftly. 'Because if he loves me he will accept me and know and understand my values. And besides…' She stopped, her face burning as she realised just how close she had come to telling him that the fact that she had so far not met such a man and was still a virgin would tell its own story to the man who eventually claimed her love. 'Why are you asking me all these questions?' she demanded sharply instead.

'No reason,' he replied laconically.

Through the darkness Petra could sense him evaluating her.

'So,' he announced at last. 'You are offering to pay me five thousand pounds to pursue and seduce you and publicly ruin your reputation.'

'To pretend to,' Petra corrected him immediately.

'What's wrong?' he taunted her. 'Having second thoughts?'

'Certainly not!' Petra denied indignantly, and then gasped in shock as he closed the distance between them and took her in his arms, demanding shakily, 'What are you doing?'

He smelled of clean night air and warm male skin, of the dangerous heat of the desert and the cool mystery of the night, and her whole body quivered in helpless reaction to his maleness. The slow descent of his head blocked out the light and the glitter of his eyes mesmerised her into unmoving stillness.

'We have made a pact! A bargain!' she felt him murmuring against her lips.

'And now we must seal it. In the desert in times gone by such things were sealed in blood. Shall I prick your skin and release the life blood from your veins, to mingle it with my own, or will this suffice?'

Before Petra could protest his mouth was on her own, crushing the breath from her lungs. Oh yes, she had been right, she recognised weakly. He was as swift and as deadly as the panther she had mentally likened him to earlier...

A tiny frantic moan bubbled in her throat as she felt her body's helpless response to the mastery of his kiss. She had been right to fear the passionate expertise indicated by that full bottom lip. There was a slight roughness about his face that chafed slightly against her own soft skin, and she had to fight to control the instinctive movement of her hand towards his face to touch that distinctive maleness. As he released her lips it seemed for some inexplicable shaming reason that they were determined to cling to his. Panic flooded over her, and before she could stop herself she bit fiercely into his lip in defiant pride.

The shock of the taste of his blood on her tongue held her immobile.

As she tensed herself for his retaliation she felt his hand wrapping round the slenderness of her throat.

'So…you prefer to seal our bargain in blood after all? There is more of the desert in you than I had realised.'

And then before she could move his mouth was on hers again, crushing it with the pressure of a kind of kiss that was totally outside anything she had ever experienced. She could taste his blood, feel the rough velvet of his tongue, hear the frenzy of a desert storm in her own heartbeat and the relentless, unforgiving burn of its sun in the touch of his hand against her throat.

And then abruptly he had released her, and as he raised his head for a brief moment Petra saw his face fully illuminated for the first time.

His eyes were open and shock reeled through her as she discovered that they were not, after all, as she had imagined dark brown, but a pure, clear, cool, steely silver-grey.

'We have the whole morning at our disposal, Petra. I thought you might like to go shopping. There is an exclusive shopping centre nearby, which has some wonderful designer shops, and…'

With a tremendous effort Petra tried to concentrate on what her aunt was saying to her.

She had telephoned Petra the previous evening to suggest that she show her something of the city and its shops. Whatever she thought about her grandfather's behaviour, Petra could not help but like her aunt by marriage—even if she had been the one to speak to Petra self-consciously the very day her godfather had left.

'Your grandfather knows how disappointed you must be that his doctor's orders mean that he is unable to see you just yet, Petra, and so he has arranged for a…a family friend who…who has a major financial interest in it, to give you a guided tour of the hotel complex and to show something of our country. You will like Rashid. He is a very charming and very well-educated man.'

Petra had had to bite on her tongue to prevent herself from bursting out angrily that she knew exactly who and what Rashid was—thanks to Saud's innocent revelations!

She had been awake for what felt like virtually the whole of the night, reliving over and over again those moments on the beach and wondering how she could ever have been stupid enough to allow them to happen, and had then fallen into a deep sleep which had left her feeling heavy-eyed.

The combination of that and the nervous edginess that was making her start at every tiny sound had exhausted her, and shopping was the last thing she felt like doing. Besides, what if *he* should try to get in touch with her? Would he do that, or would he expect her to seek him out on the beach and perhaps throw herself at him in the same shameless way she had heard that the other women had done? The thought made her stomach tense nauseously. No, their arrangement was that he was the one who had to pursue her, she reminded herself. Pursue and seduce her, a tiny inner voice whispered dangerously to her...

Seduce her. A fierce shudder ran through her, causing her aunt to ask in concern if she was cold.

'Cold? In nearly thirty degrees of heat?' Petra laughed. Her aunt might protest that in Zuran it was winter, but to Petra it felt blissfully warm.

'Your grandfather hopes to be well enough to see you very soon,' her aunt continued. 'He is very much looking forward to that, Petra. He keeps asking if you look anything like your mother...'

Petra tried not to be affected by her aunt's gentle words. 'If he really wanted to know he could have found out a long time ago—when my mother was still alive,' she pointed out, remaining unforgiving.

It was so tempting to tell her aunt that she knew the real reason she was here in Zuran, but she had no wish to get her young cousin into trouble.

'What do you think of the hotel complex?' her aunt was asking her, tactfully changing the subject.

Petra toyed with the idea of fibbing but her conscience refused to allow her to do so.

'It's…it's breathtaking,' she admitted. 'I haven't explored all of it yet, of course. After all it's almost like a small town. But what I have seen…'

She particularly liked the traditional design of the interconnecting hotel and villa complexes, with their private courtyards filled with sweetly scented plants and fruit trees, and the musical sound of fountains which had reminded Petra immediately of both the Moorish style of Southern Spain's architecture and images her mother had shown her as a child of Arabian palaces.

'When Rashid shows you round you must tell him that. Although unfortunately it may be several days before he is able to do so. He sent word to your grandfather this morning that he has been called away on business on behalf of The Royal Family… Another project he is working on in the desert.'

'He works?' Petra made no attempt to conceal her disbelief. From what Saud had told her, her prospective suitor sounded far too wealthy and well-connected to do something so mundane.

'Oh, yes,' her aunt assured her. 'As well as having a large financial interest in this complex he also designed it. He is a very highly qualified architect and greatly in demand. He trained in England. It was his mother's wish that he should go to school there, and after her death his father honoured that wish.'

An architect! Petra frowned, but she had no intention of showing any interest in a man she had already decided to despise.

'It sounds as though he is a very busy man,' she told her aunt. 'There really is no need for him to give up his time to show me round the complex. I am perfectly capable of exploring it on my own.'

'No. You must not do that,' her aunt protested once they were on their own again.

'No? Then perhaps Saud could accompany me?' Petra could not resist teasing her.

'No…no! It is best that Rashid should show you. After all, he is the one who designed the complex and he will be able to answer any questions you might have.'

'And his wife?' Petra questioned innocently. 'Will she not mind him spending his precious free time with me?'

'Oh, he is not married,' her aunt assured her immediately. 'You will like him, Petra,' she assured her enthusiastically. 'You have much in common with one another, and—' She broke off as her mobile phone started to ring.

Her aunt reached beneath her robes to retrieve her phone. But as Petra listened to her speaking quickly in Arabic, she saw her aunt's face crease in anxiety. 'What is it?' she demanded as soon as the call was over. 'Is it my grandfather? Is he—'

Furious with herself for her unguarded reaction, and for her concern, Petra stopped speaking and bit her lip.

'That was your uncle,' her aunt told her. 'Your grandfather has suffered a relapse. He knows that he has been ordered to rest but he will not do so! I must go home, Petra. I am sorry.'

Just for a moment Petra was tempted to plead to be allowed to go with her—to be allowed to see her grandfather, the closest person to her in blood she had—but quickly she stifled her weakening and unwanted emotions. Her grandfather meant nothing to her. How could he when she so obviously meant nothing to him? She must not forget the past and his plans for her. No, she was certainly not going to be the one to beg to see him. Her mother had begged and pleaded and had suffered the pain of being ignored and rejected. There was no way that she, Petra, was going to allow her grandfather to do the same to her!

After a taxi had dropped her off outside the hotel, Petra made her way into the lobby. With the rest of the day to herself there were any number of things Petra knew she could do.

The complex had its own *souq,* filled with craftspeople making and selling all manner of deliciously irresistible and traditional things, or she could leave the hotel and enjoy a gondola ride through the man-made canals that bisected the complex, or walk in the tranquillity of its gardens. And of course she could simply chill out if she so wished, either by one of the several stunningly designed pools, including a state-of-the-art 'horizon pool', or even on one of the private beaches that belonged to the complex.

The pools and beaches were reached via a man-made 'cave' below the lobby floor of the hotel, where it was possible to either walk or be taken in one of the resort's beach buggies.

Once there, as Petra had already discovered, a helpful employee would carry her towel to the lounger of her choice, and position both it and her beach umbrella for her before summoning a waiter in case she wanted to order a drink.

Nothing that a guest might need, no matter how small—

or how large—had been left to chance in the planning of the complex or the training of its staff. Petra had travelled all over the world, both with her parents, her godfather, and on her own, and she had already decided that she had never visited anywhere where a holidaymaker's needs were catered for so comprehensively and enthusiastically as they were here.

But of course she was not here on holiday—even if her closest girlfriends at home had insisted on dragging her round some of London's top stores before she had left, to equip her with a suitably elegant wardrobe for her trip.

Baring in mind her own innate modesty, and the country she was travelling to, Petra had eschewed the more *outré* samples of resort wear her enthusiastic friends had pointed out to her—although from what she had seen of her fellow holidaymakers' choice she could have chosen the briefest and most minimal bikini and still have felt comparatively over-dressed compared with some of them.

Instead she had opted for cool, elegant linens and discreet tankini beach sets, plus several evening outfits including an impossible to resist designer trouser suit in a wonderfully heavy cream matt silk satin fabric, which the salesgirl and her friends had tried in vain to convince her she should wear with simply the one-button jacket fastened over her otherwise naked top half.

'You've got the figure for it,' the salesgirl had urged her, and her friends had wickedly agreed. But Petra had refused to give in, and so a simple cream silk vest with just a hint of a pretty gold thread running through it had been added to her purchases.

A rueful smile quirked her mouth as she remembered the more outrageous of her two friends attempts to persuade her to buy a trendy outfit they had seen in a London department store: a fringed and tasselled torso-baring top, with a pair of matching lower than hip level silky pants which had revealed her belly button, claiming mock innocently that it would be perfect for her to wear in a country that celebrated the art of belly dancing.

Petra had known when she was being wound up. Her smile deepened as she instinctively touched her smooth flat stomach with her fingertips. Hidden beneath her clothes was the discreet little diamond navel stud she had bought herself just before she'd left home to replace the one she had been wearing whilst her recently pierced flesh had healed up.

No one, not even her friends, knew of the uncharacteristic flash of reckless defiance which had led to her having her navel pierced the very day after her godfather had finally ground down her opposition and persuaded her to come to Zuran.

Secretly Petra had to acknowledge that there was something dangerously decadent and wanton about the way the tiny diamond she had bought for herself flashed whenever it caught the light, but of course no one was ever likely to see it, or to know of her rebellious emotional reaction at having to give in to her grandfather's desire for her to visit his country.

Thinking of her grandfather made Petra frown. Just how serious was his heart condition? She had assumed from her uncle's original calm, almost casual reference to it that it was not a particular cause for concern.

Was he as ill as her aunt seemed to believe? Or was it simply a ploy, a means of manipulating her and putting pressure on her? Petra was fiercely determined that she would not give one inch to the despot who had caused her mother so much pain, and she was convinced that he was playing the kind of cat and mouse game that her mother had often told her he was an expert at, using his supposed poor health as a means of keeping her in dark about his real plans for her. Naturally such behaviour on his part had put her on her mettle and alerted her most defensive and hostile reactions. But what if she had been wrong? What if her grandfather was genuinely very ill?

Although it would have been impossible for her not to be emotionally touched by the warmth of her aunt and uncle's reception of her, and their concern that she might be disappointed at being deprived of what they seemed to assume was a much longed for meeting with her grandfather, Petra's antipathy towards her grandfather had been intensified by his emotional manipulation and had caused her to harden her heart even more against him.

She had every right to both mistrust and dislike him, she reassured herself. So why was she feeling somehow abandoned and rejected—excluded from the anxious family circle which had gathered protectively around him? Why did she feel this sense of anxiety and urgency to know what was going on? Why did she feel this sense of pain and loss?

Her uncle or her aunt would ring her at the hotel if they thought it was necessary; she knew that. But that wasn't like being there, being part of what was happening, being totally accepted.

A family walked past her in the foyer, on their way to the piano lounge, its three generations talking happily together. A deep sense of anguish welled up dangerously inside Petra. Grimly she tried to suppress what she was feeling. She had always been too vulnerable to her emotions. Her Celtic inheritance was responsible for that! Against her will she discovered that she was remembering how she had felt as a child, knowing that she was different, sensing her mother's pain and helpless to do anything to alleviate it, envious of other children she knew who talked easily and confidently about their adoring grandparents.

She was letting her feelings undermine her common sense, she warned herself. Her grandfather had only brought her here for one reason and it had nothing to do with adoring her! To him she was merely a suddenly valuable pawn in the intricate game he so enjoyed playing with other people's lives, using them to advance his own lust for power.

But if he was ill...seriously ill...if...something should happen before she had the chance to meet him....

Swallowing against the sharp lump in her throat, Petra headed for the lift. She would go upstairs to her room and decide how she was going to spend the rest of the day.

The suite her family had booked her in to was elegantly luxurious and large enough to house a whole family. Not only did it have a huge bathroom, complete with the largest shower Petra had even seen, as well as a sunken whirlpool bath, it also had a separate wardrobe-filled dressing room, and a bedroom with the most enormous bed she had even slept in, as well as a private terrace overlooking one of the complex's enclosed gardens.

Letting herself into the suite, Petra walked over to the dressing table and put down her bag. As she did so she glanced into the mirror and then froze as in it she saw the reflection of the bed—and more importantly the man lounging on it: her would-be seducer and partner in crime! His hands were clasped behind his head as he watched her, his body covered in nothing more than the towel he had wrapped around his hips. Tiny drops of moisture still glinting on his skin testified to the fact that he must have only recently stepped out of the shower—her shower, Petra reminded herself, unable to stop her eyes widening in betraying shock as she turned round and stared at him in disbelief.

Her suite, like the others on the same floor, and like the palatial owners suite above them, could only be reached by a private lift for which one needed a separate security card!

But for a man like this one anything and everything was possible, Petra suspected.

Like someone in a trance, she watched as he swung his feet to the floor and stood up.

If that towel he had wrapped so precariously around his body should slip...

Nervously she wetted her suddenly dry lips with the tip of her tongue. His own mouth, she suddenly realised on a flush of dangerous raw heat, bore a small fresh scar. Mesmerised, she tried to drag her gaze away from it...from him...

Had someone turned off the air-conditioning? she wondered dizzily. The room suddenly seemed far too warm...

He was walking towards her now, and in another few seconds... Automatically she backed away.

CHAPTER THREE

As THOUGH it was someone else who was actually speaking, Petra heard her own voice, thick and openly panicky, demanding, 'What are you doing in here?'

She could have sworn that her nervousness was amusing him. There was quite definitely a distinct glint in his eyes as he replied easily, 'Waiting for you, of course.'

'In here and…and like that?' Petra couldn't stop the indignation from wobbling her voice. 'What if someone else had been with me…my aunt…?'

Carelessly he gave a small shrug.

'Then you would have achieved your purpose, wouldn't you? Besides, we needed to talk, and I needed to shower, so it made sense for me to deal with both those needs together.'

He looked so totally at home in her suite that she felt as though she was the interloper, Petra acknowledged, and she wasn't even going to begin to ask just how he had managed to gain access to it.

'You could have showered in your own accommodation,' she told him primly. 'And as for us talking—I had planned to come down to the beach later.'

'Later would have been too late,' he told her. 'This is my afternoon off. And as for my own accommodation—' he gave her a wry look '—do you honestly suppose that the hotel staff are housed as luxuriously as its guests?'

Petra's throat had gone dry—not, she quickly assured herself, because of that sudden and unwanted mental image she had just had of him standing beneath the warm spray of the shower…his naked body gleaming taut and bronze-gold as he soaped the sculptured perfection of the six-pack stomach that was so clearly revealed by the brevity of the towel that did little more than offer the merest sop to modesty—hers and quite obviously not his, Petra reflected indignantly as he strolled round the room, patently unconcerned that the towel might slip!

'How…how did you manage to find me? I didn't tell you my name and you didn't give me yours.'

'It wasn't hard. Your grandfather is very well known.'

Petra's eyes widened. 'You know him?'

The dark eyebrows rose mockingly.

'Would a mere itinerant worker be allowed to "know" a millionaire?'

'And your name is?' Petra pressed him.

Was she imagining it, or had he frowned and hesitated rather longer than was necessary?

'It's Blaize,' he told her briefly.

'Blaize?' Petra looked at him.

'Something wrong?' he challenged her.

Petra shook her head.

'No, it—it's just that I had assumed that you must be Southern European—Italian, or…or Spanish or Greek. But your name…'

'My mother was Cornish,' he told her almost brusquely.

'Cornish?' Petra repeated, bemused.

'Yes,' he confirmed, boredom beginning to enter his voice as he informed her, 'According to my mother, her ancestors belonged to a band of wreckers!'

Wreckers. Well, that no doubt accounted for his colouring, and for that sharp air of danger and recklessness about him, Petra reasoned, remembering that Cornish wreckers were supposed to have pillaged galleons from the defeated Spanish Armada, taking from them not just gold but the high-born Spanish women who were sailing on them with their husbands as well.

Blaize. It suited him somehow. Blaize.

'So now that we've got the civilities out of the way, perhaps we can turn our attention to some practicalities. This plan of yours—'

'I don't want to discuss it now,' Petra interrupted him. 'Please get dressed and leave…'

She was beginning to feel increasingly uncomfortable, increasingly agitated and aware of the effect his virtual nudity was having on her!

'What's wrong?' he questioned her sharply. 'Have you changed your mind? Has your family perhaps managed to persuade you to consider this man they have chosen for you after all? After all, there are worse things to be endured than marriage to a very wealthy man…'

'Not so far as I am concerned,' Petra told him sharply. 'I can't imagine anything worse than…than a loveless marriage,' she told him passionately.

'Have you ever been in love?' he questioned her, answering his own question as he said softly, 'No, of course you haven't. Otherwise…'

There was a glint in his eyes that was making Petra's heart beat far too fast. She was still in shock from discovering him in her room and, even worse, her senses were still reacting to the totally relaxed and arrogant male way in which he was now lounging against the wall, arms folded across his chest, tightening the muscles in them in a way that for some reason refused to allow her to withdraw her fascinated female gaze from them.

'Whether or not I have ever been in love has nothing whatsoever to do with our…our business arrangement,' Petra reproved him sternly.

'When are you supposed to be being introduced to Rashid?'

Petra frowned. 'I…I don't know! You see at the moment I'm not even supposed to know what my grandfather has planned. My aunt has dropped several discreet hints about Rashid, pretending that he is just a kind family friend who has offered to…to show me round the complex, but…'

When Blaize's eyebrows rose, Petra explained defensively, 'It seems that he doesn't merely have a large financial interest in it, but that he helped design it as well. According to my aunt, he's a trained architect.'

Petra wondered uncomfortably if Blaize could hear the slight breathlessness in her voice. If so she hoped he would assume it was because she was impressed by her would-be suitor's academic qualifications rather than by the sight of Blaize's own muscles!

'When is he to show you around?'

Petra shrugged her shoulders.

'I don't know. According to my aunt, Rashid the Sheikh has been called away on business.'

'And you are no doubt hoping that by the time he returns enough damage will have been done to your reputation to have him questioning your suitability to be his wife? Well, if that is to be achieved we should not waste any time,' Blaize told her, without waiting for her response. 'Tonight everyone who is anyone on the Zuran social scene will be out and about, looking to see and be seen, and the current in place for that is a restaurant here on this complex called The Venue. It has a Michelin-starred chef and boasts a separate music room where diners can dance. I think that you and I should make our first public appearance there tonight. Dress is formal, and there is a strict admissions policy, but as a guest of the hotel and a woman that won't be a problem for you!'

'It sounds expensive,' Petra told him doubtfully.

'It is,' he agreed. 'But surely that isn't a problem? You did tell me that you are staying here at your family's request, and as their guest, and since the cost of dining in the restaurant can be debited to your room—'

'No! I couldn't possibly do that,' Petra denied immediately, unable to conceal either her distaste or her shock. But far from being contrite, Blaize merely looked amused.

'Why ever not? You have to eat, don't you?'

'I have to eat, yes,' Petra acknowledged. 'But I can't possibly expect my family to pay for...'

As she paused, struggling to find the right words to express her feelings, Blaize shrugged and told her bluntly, 'Either you were serious about this plan of yours or it was just a childish impulse that you're now regretting. In which case, you're wasting my time as well as your own—'

'I *am* serious,' Petra interrupted him quickly.

'Very well, then. We eat late here, so I shall meet you downstairs in the foyer at nine-thirty—unless of course you want me to come up to your room to collect you a little earlier, which would give us time to...'

'No,' Petra said firmly, her face burning as she saw the amused look he was giving her.

'How very much the epitome of a nervous virgin you look and sound right now! Are you one?'

Her face burning even hotter, Petra told him fiercely, 'You have no right to ask me that kind of question.'

Laughing softly, Blaize shook his head. 'Who would have thought it? Now you *have* surprised me! A nervous virgin who wants to be considered openly sexually available. You really don't want this marriage, do you?'

'I've just told you I am not prepared to discuss my...my personal private life with you...'

'Even though you expect me to publicly convince others

that I am very much a part of that personal private life…very, very much a part of it?' he said softly.

There was a look in his eyes that was making Petra's insides quiver with tension and indignation. How dared he make fun of her? It occurred to her that somehow or other he had managed to turn their relationship around so that he was the one who was in control of what was happening rather than her. A presentiment shiver brushed over her skin, warning her that she might be in danger of getting herself involved in a situation that she ultimately could not control. But before she could analyse her fears properly the doorbell to her suite suddenly rang, the shrilling sound activating her inner alarm system and throwing her body into immediate anxiety.

'It's okay,' Blaize informed her easily. 'That will be Room Service. I ordered something to eat.'

'*You* ordered…' Petra stared at him, and then looked frantically towards the suite door as the bell rang again. 'You can't—' she began, and then stopped, pink-cheeked, as she realised Blaize was laughing softly at her.

'You know,' he said, 'I think that this is going to be fun. Have you any idea how tempting it is to really shock you, little Miss Prim?'

Still laughing, he leaned forward and cupped her face with his hand, brushing her unsuspecting mouth with his own before releasing her and disappearing into the bathroom just before the suite door opened and the meal he had ordered was brought in.

'Panic over?'

Automatically Petra looked towards Blaize as he emerged from the bathroom, still wearing merely the towel, with an electric razor in one hand whilst he smoothed the skin of his newly shaved jaw with the other. Then she quickly looked away as her heart did a triple-flip before losing its balance and slamming heavily into her chest wall.

What on earth was the matter with her? So he was having a shave. So what?

So what? The voice of moral female indignation inside her retorted angrily; what he was doing was an act of deliberate male intimacy…shaving in her suite…in her bathroom…

'Mmm. I could get used to this,' he told her appreciatively as he studied the well-laden trolley. 'Pour me a cup of coffee, would you?' he called out to her as he turned back towards the bathroom. 'Black and strong, no sugar.'

Pour him a coffee! Who on earth did he think he was?

'Oh, by the way,' he told her, pausing as he reached the bathroom door. 'I've already booked us a table at The Venue for tonight, and told them to bill it to your room. We were lucky. They were virtually fully booked. Are you sure you don't feel like short-circuiting things? I could move in here and…'

'No!'

Petra's denial was an explosive sound of outrage and panic, but far from shaming him it just seemed to add to her tormentor's amusement.

Relaxing against the open doorway, he told her wickedly, 'You know, I think I could really enjoy making this seduction the real thing, if you want me to.'

'No.' This time her denial was even more vehement, her eyes huge and storm-lashed as she added in a strangled voice, 'Never.'

'Ah, yes! I forgot that you're saving yourself for the man of your dreams! Well, take care he doesn't turn into a nightmare… Is that my coffee?' he added easily, coming to rescue the cup that she was in danger of overfilling.

Furious with herself for her automatic response to his original request, Petra snatched the cup back from him.

'No, it isn't' she denied. 'It's mine. You can pour your own.'

Unperturbed, he shrugged and reached for the coffee pot, leaving Petra to digest her hollow victory along with the bitterly strong coffee she had claimed.

Broodingly she watched as Blaize tucked into the meal he had ordered with obvious relish. This wasn't what she had envisaged when she had initially approached him. What she had had in mind was an open and obvious flirtation on the beach, perhaps a couple of very public outings and maybe a meal together thrown in.

'Come and sit down and have something to eat. I ordered enough for both of us,' Blaize told her.

'So I see,' Petra agreed waspishly.

There was no way she could let her family pay for whatever Blaize had added to her bill. Thankfully she had come away with plenty of traveller's cheques and her credit cards, and her godfather—no doubt motivated by guilt—had pressed a very generous sum of money on her before he had left for the far east.

'I'm a working man,' Blaize told her cheerfully.

'I'm glad you reminded me,' Petra replied. 'And, talking of your work, shouldn't you…?'

'Don't worry,' he assured her. 'I had some leave owing to me, so I've arranged to take some time off. That way I can be free to do whatever you want me to do. If our Rashid is prepared to take you sight unseen, so to speak, then I dare say he's going to be pretty hard to shift. So you and I are going to have to make sure that we're convincing. Are you sure you don't want me to move in here?' he pressed, looking wistfully at her large bed.

'Perfectly sure,' Petra told him through gritted teeth.

'And just as soon as you've finished I would be grateful if you would get dressed and leave.'

'Leave? So soon? I thought we could spend some time getting to know one another a little better.'

To Petra's chagrin she knew that her expression had betrayed her even before he started to laugh.

'You're going to have to do much better than this if you expect to convince anyone that you've ever done anything more than exchange chaste kisses with a man—never mind that you and I are lovers,' he warned her when he had stopped laughing.

'The whole purpose of my paying you is that your reputation is dire enough to do the convincing for both of us!' Petra reminded him flintily.

'You look very hot and uncomfortable,' Blaize responded, ignoring both her comment and her ire. 'I can recommend the shower. In fact, if you like—'

'No! Don't you dare…' Petra stopped him, hot-cheeked.

'Dare what?' he asked her mock innocently. 'I was only going to say that I could alter the height of the shower head for you if you wanted me to.'

Petra gave him a fulminating look.

'Thank you, but I'm perfectly capable of doing that for myself,' she told him.

She bitterly regretted having let slip to him the fact that she was still a virgin. He obviously thought it hugely entertaining and would no doubt continue to goad and tease her about it. Unless she found a way of stopping him!

Petra tensed as the telephone in her suite started to ring. Before answering it she glanced at her reflection in the mirror. She had almost finished getting ready and she was wearing her new cream trouser suit. Warily she picked up the receiver, only to discover that her caller was her aunt.

'I meant to ring you earlier,' she apologised. 'Are you all right? I feel so guilty about leaving you on your own.'

As she assured her that she was fine, Petra waited for her aunt to make a firm arrangement for her to visit her family and finally meet her grandfather. But instead of issuing any invitation there was a small awkward silence from her aunt, and then an unconvincing and rushed explanation that certain family obligations meant it would not be possible for them to spend any time with her on the following day.

'At least your grandfather is feeling a little better. Although the doctor says that he must still rest. He is longing to see you, Petra, and—'

If anything her aunt's voice sounded even more unconvincing, Petra reflected bitterly.

Well she certainly wasn't going to turn herself into a liar by saying that she was longing to see *him*. She had no idea what he was hoping to achieve by what he was doing, unless it was to make her feel so isolated and alone that she practically fell into her proposed suitor's arms out of gratitude to him for rescuing her from her solitude.

'It is such a pity that my own family, my sisters and their children, are out of the country right now,' her aunt was continuing. 'But as soon as Rashid gets back—'

'You mustn't worry about me, Aunt,' Petra interrupted her. 'I am perfectly capable of entertaining myself. As a matter of fact...' Petra paused, wondering how much she ought to say.

But her aunt obviously wasn't listening properly because she cut across what Petra was saying, telling her, 'There are several escorted trips from the resort that you might enjoy taking, Petra, whilst you wait for Rashid to return. The gold *souq,* for one. Oh, I must go. I can hear your grandfather calling for me.'

There was barely time for Petra to wish her goodbye before her aunt had rung off.

As she turned towards the mirror to apply her lipstick Petra discovered that her hand was shaking slightly.

Because she was angry, she told herself—*not* because she was nervous at all at the thought of spending the evening with Blaize. She was angry because she knew instinctively that her aunt was not being entirely honest with her.

Mentally she tried to picture her grandfather, using the vivid verbal images her mother had drawn for her, and those she had gained herself from studying the robed men she had seen moving with imperious arrogance through the hotel. He would be bearded, of course, his profile hawk-like and his expression harsh, perhaps even vengeful as he confronted her, the child of the marriage he had fought against so bitterly and so unsuccessfully.

It was impossible for Petra to get her head round the mindset of a father who had turned from being protective and loving to one who refused so much as to hear his once beloved daughter's name spoken, simply because she had chosen to marry the man she loved.

In the mirror her own reflection confronted her. At home in England she was often conscious of looking out of place, her colouring and the delicacy of her fine-boned body giving her an almost exotic beauty, but here in her mother's country, conversely, she felt very Celtic.

Her mother! What would *she* think of the course of action Petra was taking? What would she think of Blaize?

Snatching up her purse, Petra refused to allow herself to pursue such potentially unsettling thoughts.

The lobby of the hotel was the busiest Petra had seen it since her arrival. A large group of designer-clad women and their male escorts were standing by the entrance to the piano lounge and Petra's eyes widened as she saw the jewellery the women were wearing.

Her own outfit was provoking a few assessing and appreciative female glances, as well as some much more openly male admiring ones, but Petra was unaware of them as she looked round anxiously for Blaize.

'There you are. I was just about to come up and collect you.'

Whirling round, Petra rounded her eyes as she stared at Blaize. He was dressed formally in clothes she immediately recognised as being the very best in Italian tailoring, and which she knew must have cost a small fortune. No wonder more than one of the diamond-decked women were studying him with such open sexual interest!

On the wages he must earn there was no way he could possibly afford such clothes, Petra decided, which must mean...

She didn't like the unpleasant cold feeling invading her stomach, or the lowering realisation that she was probably far from being the first woman to pay Blaize for his 'services'—although of course the services she was paying him for were no doubt very different from those normally expected by his benefactresses.

'What's wrong? You look as though you've just swallowed something extremely unpleasant.'

His intuitiveness triggered a sharp spiral of warning.

'I was just wondering what's going to be on the menu tonight,' she replied smoothly.

He might have caught her off guard this afternoon, but tonight was going to be different. This time she was going to make it plain to him that *she* was the one in charge of events and not him!

'These days Zuran is renowned for the variety and standard of its restaurants, as you are about to discover.'

As he spoke he was guiding her across the foyer, one hand protectively beneath her elbow. Petra would have liked to pull away, to put some distance between them, but the crush of people in the lobby made it impossible, and besides, she firmly reminded herself, the whole point of being with him was that she was *seen* to be with him!

However, instead of heading for the exit, as she had expected him to do, Petra discovered that he was guiding her in the direction of the large glass doors that opened out into one of the formal garden courtyards, beyond which lay the largest of the network of canals which criss-crossed the complex.

'I thought we were going out to dinner,' she said, hanging back a little as two uniformed men held open the doors for them.

'We are,' Blaize told her, giving her a quizzical look as he ushered her outside. 'What's wrong?' he teased her. 'Did you think I was taking you out into the courtyard so that I could indulge in a little private tuition before we faced our public?'

He laughed softly, the hand which had been beneath her elbow suddenly grasping her upper arm and holding her so close to his own body that she could feel the laughter vibrating as they walked out into the heavy satin warmth of the indigo-dark night.

'In a garden? Where anyone might see us. Oh, no... If *that* was my intention I would have taken you somewhere far, far more private...'

'Like your official accommodation, you mean?' Petra challenged him bitingly, determined not to let him think that she was in the least bit affected by what he was saying.

'You remind me of a little cat, all sharp claws and defensive temper. Take care that you don't tempt me to teach you how to purr with pleasure and use those claws only in the heat of passion…'

'We aren't in public, yet,' was all Petra could think of to say in retaliation and she mentally blessed the darkness for concealing her hectically flushed face. 'So you can save the practised seduction scenario until we are!'

They had almost crossed the garden now, and the canal lay in front of them. As they reached it Blaize raised his hand to summon one of the gondoliers waiting several yards away.

'This isn't the quickest way to reach the restaurant, but I think it is certainly the most…relaxing,' he informed her in a soft murmur as the gondola was brought to a halt in front of them.

As Blaize helped her into the gondola Petra wondered helplessly if anything could possibly be more romantic— or more hackneyed!

Clever lighting had transformed the daytime appearance of the resort into a place of magic and mystery, designed to appeal to the senses. Strawberry-scented vapour floated over their heads in a pale pink cloud, and in the distance Petra could see and hear fireworks. As they passed the *souq,* a fire-eater performed for a watching group of teenagers whilst a 'merchant' loaded his wares onto a waiting camel train, causing Petra's heart to give a small unsteady thump.

The one thing she wanted to do whilst she was in Zuran was take a trip into the desert. Her aunt might speak enthusiastically about shopping malls and the fabulous gold and diamond *souq,* but it was the desert that called most strongly to Petra in a siren song that whispered to her that to know it was her heritage.

Deep in her own private thoughts, she jumped when Blaize touched her arm. The gondola swung into an ornately decorated private landing from which a red carpet led towards a building so unmistakably Parisian in concept that Petra could only stare at it in bemusement.

Several other people were already standing in front of the entrance to the restaurant, and as she felt Blaize's hands on her body when he helped her from the gondola Petra immediately tensed in rejection of the sexual intimacy, instinctively uncomfortable about other people witnessing it.

'Don't do that!' she protested when Blaize bent his head and allowed his breath to graze intimately against her skin as he brushed her hair from her face. 'The women who paid for your clothes might have enjoyed being pawed in public, but I don't.'

The minute she had finished speaking Petra knew that she had gone too far. It was there in the sudden stiffening of his body and the glacial glitter in his eyes.

It was useless to try to explain that her own panic at her body's helpless reaction to him had motivated her rash words—and besides, her pride would not allow her to do so. So Petra tensed and bent her head beneath the savage lash of his softly spoken retaliation.

'For your information no woman has ever…ever…paid for my clothes. And as for your comment about "pawing"—be thankful that your innocence protects you from the consequences of such a comment—for now!'

In silence, but with her head held high, Petra turned towards the red carpet. Not for anything was she going to admit—even to herself—how much she longed for the protective warmth of Blaize's hand beneath her elbow as she watched the other diners entering the restaurant, the men in their robes and their women couturier-clad and holding themselves with a proud elegance Petra secretly envied.

'More wine?' Blaize asked as their waiter hovered solicitously, holding the wine bottle. Immediately Petra shook her head and covered her still half-full glass with her hand. The meal they had just been served had been outstandingly good—with every mouthful Petra had been reminded of her first grown-up meal in Paris, a birthday treat from her parents. Everything from the decor and the whole ambience of the place, right down to the subtle perfume of the candles on the tables, replicated the chicest of Parisian restaurants, and Petra knew she would not have been surprised to hear French itself being spoken.

'Coffee, then?' Blaize was asking as he signalled her refusal to the hovering waiter.

Nodding her head, Petra warned herself that if she was not careful she might be in danger of falling for her own fiction, so well was Blaize playing the part of attentive and adoring lover. But then, of course, no doubt he had had plenty of practice, she reminded herself grimly.

Petra dreaded to think about the impact the cost of the meal was going to make on her credit card, but there was no way she could feel comfortable allowing it to be debited to her suite.

As she waited for the waiter to bring her coffee she was suddenly aware of being studied by the occupants of a nearby table—a group of three couples.

The arrival of the waiter with her coffee momentarily distracted her, but as she glanced away from them Petra could have sworn that Blaize gave the tiniest warning shake of his head when one of the men started to get up, as though he was about to come over to their table.

As soon as the waiter had gone, Petra demanded, 'Who is that…?'

'Who do you mean?' Blaize questioned her, frowning slightly.

'The man you just looked at,' Petra said. 'He was about to come over, but you—'

'I didn't look at anyone,' Blaize denied.

'Yes, you did,' Petra insisted. 'I saw you…'

'You're imagining things,' Blaize told her. 'Which man do you mean? Point him out to me.'

Irately Petra did so, but when Blaize looked deliberately in his direction the man Petra had pointed out looked pointedly through them before averting his gaze.

Giving her an ironic look, Blaize shrugged his shoulders meaningfully whilst Petra's face burned. She had obviously been wrong after all, but she wasn't going to give Blaize the satisfaction of admitting it!

'When you have finished your coffee perhaps you would like to dance,' Blaize suggested. 'After all, we are supposed to be lovers, despite that virginal look of yours…'

Petra's mouth compressed and she put down her coffee cup with a small clatter.

'That's it!' she told him forcefully. 'From now on every time you so much as mention my…my…the word "virgin" I shall fine you five pounds, and deduct the money from your fee! I am paying you to help me escape from a marriage I don't want. Not to…to keep on bringing up something which has nothing whatsoever to do with our business arrangement!'

'No? I beg to differ,' Blaize informed her softly. 'I am supposed to create the impression that I am seducing you,' he reminded her. 'Who is going to believe that if you insist on looking like a—'

'Five pounds,' Petra warned him.

'Like a woman who does not know what it is to experience a man's passion,' Blaize finished silkily.

She had finished her coffee and Blaize had summoned the waiter to ask for the bill.

Immediately Petra reached for her bag to remove her credit card.

'What are you doing?' Blaize demanded curtly, when he saw what she was doing.

'I can't let my family pay for this. It would be… immoral…' Petra told him.

'Immoral… To allow them to pay for a meal? But not apparently immoral to allow them to believe that you are sleeping with me…a man you picked up on the beach…'

'My body is mine to do with as I wish,' Petra hissed furiously to him as the waiter arrived with the bill. She already had her credit card in her hand, but to her disbelief before she could place it on the saucer Blaize had picked up the bill.

'I shall deal with this,' he told her coolly, 'You may reimburse me later.'

Turning to the discreetly waiting waiter, he murmured something to him that Petra couldn't catch, handing the man the bill which he immediately walked away with.

Several minutes later, as they made their way to the separate music room, Petra felt as though everyone else in the restaurant was watching them. She was being over-sensitive, of course. She knew that. No doubt it was only the female diners who were watching Blaize, she told herself wryly.

The music room and its dance floor were very dimly lit, and as she heard the provocative strains of the sensual music that was being played, watched the way the dancers already on the floor were moving, she automatically pulled back. This wasn't dancing. It was…it was sex on the dance floor—and there was no way *she* was going to allow Blaize to hold *her* like that. No way she dared allow him to hold her like that.

Why not? It wasn't, after all, as though he was her type,

she reminded herself robustly, and she knew that no matter how outwardly sensual and romantic he might appear he felt nothing whatsoever for her. They were here for a purpose, and the sooner it was achieved the sooner she would be free to return home.

Squaring her shoulders, she allowed Blaize to guide her towards the dance floor.

Seconds later, held in his arms, her face pressed into his shoulder whilst his hand smoothed its way down her back, coming to rest well below her waist, Petra acknowledged that she had perhaps been over-confident about her ability to control her body's physical reaction to him.

He was a practised seducer, she told herself in her own defence. A man who had perfected his seduction technique on an unending stream of women…

'Relax… We're supposed to be lovers, remember…'

'I am relaxed,' Petra told him through gritted teeth.

'No, you aren't!' he corrected her. 'You're petrified that I'm going to do something like this to you…'

As he finished speaking he slid his hand into the hair at the nape of her neck, gently tugging her head so that his lips could graze along her throat and then nibble tormentingly against her ear. Just the feel of his breath made her whole body quiver in shocked delight as his thumb tracked the betraying pulse beating increasingly fast at the base of her throat.

'Have you any idea how very, very much I want you…?'

The throaty words he whispered against her mouth caused Petra's eyes to widen—until she remembered that he was simply acting…playing the part she was paying him to play.

'Shall I take you back to your room and show you how much? Remove the clothes from your delectable sexy body and stroke and kiss every inch of it before—'

Petra gasped as he reached for her hand and told her rawly, 'Feel what you're doing to me...'

She tried to pull free but it was too late. He was already placing her hand against his body, and she could feel the heavy thud of his heart against her palm.

'Come closer to me,' he said, drawing her deeper into his embrace, and then whispering, 'Closer than that! So close that I can pretend I have you naked in my arms, your silky skin next to mine...'

Petra knew that the heat filling her could not be blamed on the lack of air in the room, but stubbornly she refused to acknowledge what was really causing both it and the shivery, achy, tight pangs of longing that were running riot inside her body, inciting a rebellion she was terrified she might not be able to control.

Somehow she managed to put enough distance between them, to raise her head and tell him huskily, 'I want to leave.'

'So soon? It's only just gone midnight?'

Petra could feel her panic increasing. If he kept her here on the dance floor, holding her the way he was, for very much longer— It was all very well for her brain to know that he was simply acting, but her body seemed to be finding it almost impossible to differentiate between fact and fiction. It was responding to him as though...as though... she...actually wanted him!

'It's been a long day, and my aunt will probably be telephoning me early in the morning to update me on my grandfather's condition!'

'I thought you weren't interested in his health.'

'I'm not,' Petra denied immediately. 'It's just...'

Blaize had released her now, and was standing in front of her searching her face with far too sharp a gaze. Instinctively Petra wanted to hide herself—and her feelings—from him—to protect herself from something, someone she was rapidly coming to realise might potentially offer a far more serious threat to her future happiness than she felt comfortable acknowledging.

Why was he affecting her like this? After all, he wasn't the first male she had danced intimately closely with, or been kissed by; he was not even the first male who had caused her to want him! She might not as yet have had a lover, but she knew what it was to feel desire, to feel emotionally drawn to someone. She had gone through all the normal early teenage crushes on a variety of male icons, from popstars to football heroes, and she had even fancied herself in love a couple of times. But this was the first time she had been so powerfully and intimately aroused that she felt in fear of not being able to control those feelings!

'It's just what?' Blaize prompted her, breaking into her anxious thoughts.

'I don't want to talk about it,' Petra replied, stubbornly shaking her head.

'Very well, then. If you're sure you want to leave, and you're not just making an excuse to escape from my arms because you're afraid that you might enjoy being there too much...'

Petra glared at him, outwardly angry but inwardly horrified by his insouciant comment. He was probably just testing her...teasing her, she reassured herself. After all, he couldn't possible know what she was feeling...could he?

'Oh, I could never do that,' she told him firmly, giving him a carefully manufactured smile as she added sweetly, 'After all, I've never liked crowds!'

She had expected her put-down to silence him, but instead he simply demanded softly, 'Meaning?'

'Meaning that the space within your arms is crowded

with the women who have already been there,' Petra answered him forthrightly.

However, instead of being abashed, Blaize simply shrugged and told her carelessly, 'I am thirty-four years old. Naturally there have been...relationships...'

It was on the tip of Petra's tongue to tell him that it wasn't his 'relationships' she was referring to, but the other women whom she suspected had paraded in and out of his life—and his arms—in an unending and highly impermanent line. But instead she simply shook her head and started to walk away from him.

He caught up with her by the door, just as the doorman and his uniformed attendants sprang into action—almost as though they were royalty, Petra thought as she stepped onto the red carpet which led from the restaurant door to the pathway and the car park and canal.

'I think I'd rather be driven back,' Petra announced hurriedly. There was no way, in her present vulnerable mood, that she wanted to share the intimacy of a moonlit gondola ride back to her hotel with Blaize!

She had half expected him to talk her out of her decision, but instead he simply raised his hand to summon one of the waiting buggies.

Their silent return to the hotel was somehow more unnerving for Petra than even those moments on the dance floor. She couldn't understand how it was that a man in Blaize's position, who behaved as he did and who was after all being paid by her, could somehow manage to be so convincingly autocratic and superior!

Once inside the hotel, as he pressed the bell for the lift for her, Blaize told her firmly, 'The more obviously we are seen in public together, the better. So tomorrow I suggest that we make arrangements to that end. There are several organised trips we could take together.'

'Organised trips?' Petra interrupted him, frowning. 'But surely it won't be enough for you to simply be seen with me by my fellow visitors? We need to be seen together by people who are known to Rashid.'

'Zuran is a small place. I am sure that our… friendship…will soon come to his ears,' Blaize replied as the lift arrived.

He stepped into it with her and pressed the button for her floor.

'You don't need to come up with me,' Petra protested immediately, but the doors had already closed and the lift was in motion.

'What is it you are so afraid of?' Blaize mocked her when the lift had stopped. 'That I might kiss you, or that I might not?'

'Neither!' Petra denied forcefully.

'Liar!' Blaize taunted her softly. 'You are a woman, after all, and of course you want—'

'What I want,' Petra interrupted him angrily outside her suite door, 'is for you to remember that I am paying you to act as my lover in public, and that is all!'

As she spoke she was fumbling in her bag for her key card, thankfully finding it and swiping it.

Blaize's hand was on the door handle and Petra held her breath as he pushed the door open. What would she do if he insisted on coming into her room? If he insisted on doing even more than that? Her heart suddenly seemed to have developed an over-fast and erratic heartbeat, and instinctively Petra put her hand on her chest, as if she was trying to steady it.

As he held open the door for her Blaize switched on the suite lights. Petra's mouth felt dry, her body boneless and soft, the blood running hotly through her veins. She closed her eyes and then opened them again as she heard the small but distinctive click of the suite door closing.

Whirling round, she opened her mouth to tell Blaize that she wanted him to leave, and then closed it again as she stared at the empty space between her own body and the closed door where she had expected him to be.

Blaize had gone. He had not come into her suite! He had simply closed the door and left. Which was exactly what she had wanted…wasn't it?

CHAPTER FOUR

PETRA had finished her breakfast and the waiter had cleared away the room service trolley, leaving her with a fresh pot of coffee and the newspaper she had ordered.

She had eaten her breakfast outside on her private patio, in the pleasurable warmth of the early morning sunshine, and by rights she ought to be feeling contently relaxed.

But she wasn't!

Her mobile phone started to ring and she picked it up.

'Petra?'

The unexpected sound of her godfather's voice banished her mood of introspection.

He was ringing from a satellite connection, he told her, and would not be able to stay on the line very long.

'How are you getting on with your grandfather?' he asked.

'I'm not,' Petra responded wryly. 'I haven't even seen him yet. He hasn't been well enough, apparently.'

'Petra—I can't hear you!' She heard her godfather interrupting her, his own voice so faint that she could barely hear it. 'The line's breaking up. I'm going to have to go. I'll be out of contact for the next couple of weeks. Government business…'

A series of sharp crackles distorted his voice so much that Petra couldn't make out what he was saying, although she thought he was telling her that he loved her. Before she could make any response the line had gone dead.

Miserably she stared at the now blank screen. There would be no point in her trying to ring back; she had no idea exactly where her godfather was and she didn't have a number.

It was a pity that she hadn't been able to beg him to send her her passport before the line had broken up! Now her only means of escape from her unwanted marriage was quite definitely via Blaize.

As a tiny shower of tingling excitement skittered dangerously down her spine Petra warned herself that she was being foolish—and gullible! Why had she allowed Blaize to manoeuvre her into agreeing to last night's expensive meal, when surely her purpose could have been just as easily if not even better achieved via a short interlude on the beach with him?

She glanced at her mobile. Perhaps out of good manners she ought to at least telephone to enquire after her grandfather's health. A little nervously Petra dialled the number of the family villa.

An unfamiliar male voice answered, throwing Petra into confusion. Hesitantly she asked for her aunt, and was asked for her own name. Several seconds later Petra breathed out in relief as she heard her aunt's voice.

A little uncomfortably, asked after her grandfather.

'He has had a good night,' her aunt told her. 'But he is still very weak. He insisted on going to morning prayers, although he was not supposed to do so. Unfortunately he had instructed his manservant to drive him there before I realised what was going on. I am so glad that you have rung, Petra. It will mean such a lot to him to know of your concern.'

The genuine warmth and approval in her voice was making Petra feel even more uncomfortable, and rather guilty as well, even though she tried to reassure herself that she had nothing to feel guilty about.

'You are being wonderfully patient,' her aunt continued.

'I promise you it won't be long now before you will be able to see him. I had intended to telephone you myself, to ask if you would like to go round the spice *souq* tomorrow morning, and then perhaps we could have lunch together?'

'I…that sounds very nice,' Petra accepted lamely. Feeling even more uncomfortable and guilty, she quickly ended the call.

She needed to see Blaize, she decided firmly, to make sure that he realised she was the one in charge of things and not him. He had said that he would make contact with her, but she was being driven by a sense of anxious urgency.

She wanted…needed to see Blaize now!

Half an hour later she stood on the beach, trying to cope with the frustration of explaining to the anxious to please lifeguard and the young man who was now in charge of the windsurfers what she wanted. But they didn't seem to recognise Blaize from her description, Petra slowly forced herself to count to ten.

It wasn't their fault that they didn't know Blaize! The fault lay with her, not with them, for not making sure that she was able to get in touch with him. Thanking the two young men for their attempts to help her, she made her way back to her hotel.

It was lunchtime but she wasn't really hungry; the emptiness inside her could not be satisfied with food! She had been infuriated by the way Blaize had tormented her about her virginity, and disturbed by her own physical reaction to him. Of course there was no way she had really wanted him to kiss her last night, but just supposing that he had.

Quickly Petra pressed the lift button, hoping that no one had noticed her flushed face or the fierce shudder that had gripped her body.

What on earth was the matter with her? Petra derided

herself scornfully as the lift carried her smoothly and effortlessly upwards. She might be a virgin but that did not mean she was sexually repressed or unaware—so naïve and vulnerable that all it took to arouse her was one look from a predatory experienced male!

But if Blaize *had* kissed her... If he had then she would have had the common sense to reject him and send him packing, she assured herself firmly. Theirs was a business relationship and that was the way she intended it to stay!

The lift had stopped. She got out and made her way to her suite, holding her breath as she opened the door. But this time there was no virtually naked man reclining on her bed. Much to her relief! Or so she told herself.

Half an hour later she was still trying to decide what she was going to do with the rest of her day. A little restlessly she paced her terrace. She wasn't really in the mood for the beach. The guidebook she had found suggested several walks through the city which took in various points of interest. Quickly she went to find it, picking it up and flicking through it.

There was one walk which took in the older parts of the town, including a tour of the home of a former ruler. It had now been turned into a museum documenting the social, cultural, educational and religious history of the area.

Firmly Petra told herself that it would do her good to have something other than her grandfather and the problems he was causing her to occupy her mind. After changing into a pair of white linen trousers and pulling on a loose long-sleeved cotton top, Petra left her suite.

Outside the afternoon sunshine was strong enough to have her reaching for her sunglasses whilst she waited for the concierge staff to summon her a taxi. Out of the corner of her eye she saw an immaculate shiny black stretch limousine pulling up a few yards away from her.

Curiously she watched as a flurry of anxious attendants hurried to open doors and several very important-looking robed men got out of the vehicle. Watching them discreetly, Petra suddenly stiffened, and then relaxed, shaking her head ruefully. Just for a second she had actually thought that in profile one of the robed men looked like Blaize! How ridiculous! Of course it couldn't possibly be him! It wasn't only her preoccupation with her grandfather she needed to clear out of her thoughts, she told herself grimly as she headed for her waiting taxi.

She had spent so much time inside the museum that outside it was going dark, Petra realised as she drew a deep breath of evening air into her lungs, her head full of everything she had just seen.

It wasn't just Zuran's history and past she had just experienced, it was also part of her own—which of course was why the contents of the museum had so absorbed her. Inside the museum, for the first time she had actually felt a sense of awareness and recognition of her Bedouin roots, and with that the first tentative, uncurling delicate tendrils of belonging. For the first time in her life she was actually recognising and acknowledging that she needed to know more about this country—not just for her mother's sake but for her own.

There was a faint scent on the wind that caused her to lift her head and look towards the desert. There on the wind was the scent of her past, her destiny, and instinctively her senses recognised it. She was part of a proud race of people who had roamed this land when Cleopatra had been Queen, when Marco Polo had made his epic journey along the silk road.

Without thinking about what she was doing Petra

reached down and scooped up a small handful of sand, letting it trickle slowly through her fingers. Her country...

Her eyes blurred with tears. Fiercely she blinked them away.

A group of people hurried past her, accidentally jostling her, and the mood was broken. It was almost dark and she was hungry. She hailed a cruising taxi and gave him the address of her hotel.

Hesitantly, Petra scanned the hotel foyer. She had booked herself a table for dinner at the complex's Italian restaurant, but now, standing in the foyer and realising that she was the only woman there on her own, she was beginning to have second thoughts. But Zuran was an extremely cosmopolitan and safe country, she reminded herself stoutly, and the complex was geared to the needs of the visitor—even a solitary female such as herself.

Tonight she had dressed a little less dramatically, in a simple black linen dress that buttoned down the front. Its neat square neckline showed off the delicate bones at the base of her throat and the proud arch of her neck, just as the plain gold bangle she was wearing on her wrist revealed the fragility of its bone structure. The bangle had originally belonged to her mother, and Petra touched it now, seeking its comforting reassurance.

She wasn't used to dining in public alone but she refused to eat a solitary meal in her suite!

The clerk at the hotel's guest relations desk assured her that she didn't have very far to walk to the Italian restaurant—which, he explained, was situated in its own private courtyard and could be reached on foot or by gondola.

Taking a gondola was too dangerous, Petra decided. It might remind her of last night and Blaize! She started to frown. All day she had been on edge, expecting Blaize to get in touch with her, but he had not done so. Because he had found someone more profitable to spend his time with, both financially and sexually? She had already seen that there was no shortage of admiring women eager for his company.

Pausing in mid-step, Petra firmly reassured herself that the funny little ache she was experiencing had nothing at all to do with any jealousy. Her? Jealous of Blaize's other women? How ridiculous!

The clerk had been right when he had told her that the restaurant wasn't very far away. Petra turned a corner and found herself in the courtyard he had mentioned to her.

The middle of the courtyard was filled with fountains and pools, the jets of water from them making intricate patterns suddenly broken by an unexpected powerful surge that sent one of the jets soaring into the air, much to the delight of a group of watching children who screamed and clapped their hands in excitement.

Smiling indulgently, Petra made her own way towards the restaurant.

Given her previous evening's experience, with the 'Parisian' Michelin-starred restaurant, she supposed she should have expected that the Italian trattoria would be equally authentic, and it certainly was—right down to the strolling musician and the appreciative genuinely Italian waiters, who ushered her to a table and handed her a menu.

Half an hour later, when Petra had just started to relax and feel comfortable as she sipped her wine and enjoyed the seafood starter she had ordered, the restaurant door opened and a group of brashly noisy young men burst in.

Petra could tell from the reactions of the restaurant staff that they were not entirely at ease with the loud-voiced demands of the new arrivals. To Petra, familiar with the behaviour of a certain type of European male, it was obvious that the men had been drinking. Their attitude towards the staff was bordering on the aggressive, and although none of them looked particularly intimidating they were in a pack, and like all pack animals they possessed a certain aura of volatility and danger.

They were speaking in English, demanding that they were given a table large enough to accommodate them all and refusing to listen when the *maître d'* tried to tell them that the restaurant was fully booked.

'Don't give us that, mate,' one of them objected. 'We can see for ourselves that you've got plenty of empty tables.'

Discreetly Petra affected not to notice what was going on when the waiter removed her empty plate and returned with her main course. But as she thanked him for her meal, she suddenly heard one of the men saying, 'Hey, look at that over there—the brunette sitting on her own. We'll have that table there, mate,' he continued, pointing to the empty one next to where Petra was seated.

She tensed warily. She could tell that the *maître d* was trying to persuade them to leave, but it was obvious that they had no intention of doing so. She tried not to betray her discomfort as they surged round her, sitting at three of the tables close to her own so that she was almost surrounded by them.

They were ordering more drinks whilst making crudely off-colour comments about their sexual proclivities and deliberately staring at her, trying to force her to return their eye contact.

Petra wasn't exactly frightened. She lived in London, after all, and considered herself to be relatively streetwise. But in London she would never have been eating on her own, or been in a situation which would have made her so vulnerable.

She was uncomfortably aware of the diners at the two other tables, young couples with children, getting up and leaving, whilst the raucous behaviour of the men around her became even more unpleasant.

Although she hadn't finished her meal, Petra recognised that it was impossible for her to stay. The newcomers were making no attempt to order a meal and instead were becoming even more disorderly. A bread roll flew past her head, quickly followed by another as two men on tables either side of her began to hurl them at one another.

'First to get one down her dress gets a free round!' one of the men sang out.

Petra had had enough.

As calmly as she could she stood up, but to her horror, instead of allowing her to walk past them, the men immediately surrounded her, making openly sexually suggestive comments both to her and about her to one another that made Petra's throat and face burn with disgust and anger.

She could see that the restaurant manager was on the telephone, and the *maître d'* was doing his best to assist her, begging the men to step back otherwise he would have to ask them to leave.

'Going to pick one of us, are you, sweetheart?' the most obnoxious of the gang smirked at Petra. 'Or shall we choose for you? Which one is going to be first, lads?' he demanded, turning to his friends.

The *maître d'* intervened, protesting, 'Please, gentlemen, I must ask you to leave—'

'We aren't going anywhere, mate,' Petra's tormentor told him drunkenly.

'Oh, but I think you are...'

The coolly incisive sound of Blaize's voice cut through

the loud-mouthed vulgarities like tempered steel slicing into flaccid flesh, his appearance shocking Petra even more than it obviously did the gang.

Instinctively she turned towards him, her expression betraying both her disbelief and her fear.

'In fact, I think I can safely say that not only are you going to leave the restaurant, you are going to leave the country as well.'

One of the gang started to laugh.

'Come off it, mate. You can't make us do anything! There's only one of you and a dozen or us, and besides…we're here for the races, see.'

'The restaurant manager has already summoned the police,' Blaize informed them coolly. 'There is a law in this country against men harassing women, and in Zuran laws are reinforced.'

Petra could hear sounds of new arrivals outside the restaurant, and it was obvious so could the gang.

Suddenly they began to look a lot less sure of themselves. Blaize was holding out his hand to her. Shakily Petra pushed her way past the men and went to his side, just as the restaurant door opened and several stern-looking uniformed police officers came in.

'Come on,' Blaize instructed Petra, taking hold of her arm. 'Let's get out of here…'

Petra was only too glad to do so. And only too glad of the protection of his firm grasp on her arm as he ushered her back to her hotel.

She could see the grim look on his face, and the way that his mouth had compressed, somehow making him look very austere and stern.

Once they were inside the hotel, Petra thought she saw him give a small curt nod in the direction of the guest relations desk and the clerk seated there, but as he bustled her towards the lift she decided that she must have imagined it.

As the lift moved upward, Petra expelled a small shaky sigh of relief.

'You don't know how pleased I was to see you—' she began, but Blaize stopped her, his expression forbiddingly grim.

'What the hell where you doing?' he demanded furiously. 'Why didn't you leave? Surely you must have realised…'

The unexpected harshness of his attack coupled with its unfairness shocked her into silence.

The lift stopped and they both got out. Her legs, Petra discovered, were trembling and she felt slightly sick.

Outside her suite, she tried to open her bag to find her key card, but her fingers were shaking so much she dropped it. As she bent down to retrieve it Blaize beat her to it, picking up her bag and opening it. Absently Petra noticed how tiny it looked in his hands. He had well-groomed nails, immaculately clean, and his fingers were long and lean. The fleshy pad just below his thumb mesmerised her, and she couldn't stop staring at it.

Distantly a part of her recognised that she was probably in shock, but that knowledge was too far away and vague for her to really comprehend it. Instead she simply accepted it gratefully as a rational explanation for the tremors that were now beginning to visibly shake her body, and the tight, aching pain that was locking her throat and preventing her from defending herself.

'Do you realise what could have happened if the manager hadn't…?'

'I tried to leave,' Petra told him, suddenly managing to speak. 'But they wouldn't let me.'

They were in the suite and the door was closed. Her

shock suddenly accelerated out of the distance and rico-
cheted towards her. Tears flooded her eyes and her body
shook violently.

'Petra!'

Now the anger she could hear in Blaize's voice sounded
different.

'Petra!'

As he repeated her name he made a sound, somewhere
between a groan and a growl and then suddenly he was
holding her in his arms.

Valiantly Petra forced back her tears. She could feel
Blaize's hand stroking her hair. Tilting back her head, she
looked up at him, and kept on looking, drowning in the
molten mercury glow of his eyes as her lips parted and her
head fell aback against his supporting arm.

'Petra…'

As he lowered his head she could feel the warmth of his
breath tantalising the quivering readiness of her lips. She
had wanted this…him…from the moment she had walked
into her room the previous day and seen him lying on her
bed, she acknowledged dizzily, as she breathed in and felt
the hard pressure of his mouth against her own.

Passion! It was just a word! How could it possibly convey all that she was feeling, all she was experiencing—
every nuance of sensation and emotion that burned and
ached through her as his mouth moved over her own, taking
her deeper and deeper into a world of dark velvet forbidden
pleasure?

There was nothing to warn her when the protective inner
barriers she had erected against him came tumbling down—
no flash of insight, no mental alarm call, no frantic conscience voice. Nothing to impede the delirious intoxication
of her senses running wild, her body clamouring for the
freedom to express its longings!

She could feel his lips moving against her mouth and then her ear as he spoke to her warningly. 'You're in shock, Petra, and this isn't—'

Frantically Petra blotted out what he was trying to say, closing her ears to it and then closing his mouth as she placed her hand against his jaw, moved her mouth back to his, her lips eagerly showing him what she wanted.

She felt him stiffen, heard his indrawn breath and held her own, suddenly sharply aware of his hesitation. But as she leaned against him, her body still trembling, but no longer out of any fear other than that he might leave her, she looked into his eyes and saw the fierce, predatory look of male hunger glittering there, and felt a sweetly powerful sense of female triumph.

She kissed him slowly, and then waited, whilst her glance slid longingly from his eyes to his mouth. Like someone in a dream she reached up and traced its shape with the tip of her finger, and caught her own bottom lip between her teeth as she felt—and saw—the shudder that rocked him.

'This isn't a good idea.' She heard him groan as he lifted her hand from his mouth and pressed a fiercely sensual kiss in its palm. Now his glance was on her face—and not just her face, she recognised as her heart gave a series of heavy, excited thuds when it dropped to her body.

'Why not?' she whispered dangerously back to him.

'Because,' he told her thickly, 'if I touch you now…here…like this…'

Petra quivered violently as his hand barely brushed against her breast and then returned to cup it gently, whilst even more tantalisingly his thumb rubbed slowly across her taut nipple.

'Then,' Blaize was continuing huskily, 'I shall need to touch you again and again, and then I will have to…'

Her flesh was melting like ice cream covered in the sensuality and irresistibility of pure hot chocolate, Petra decided, and what Blaize was doing to her was making her long to have his hands…his body against her own body. Her naked body…

The small sound of longing she made was smothered by the heat of his kiss. The sound of their mutually charged breathing filled the room, and then, disconcertingly, Petra heard the mood-destroying clatter of the fax machine. Automatically she tensed, just as Blaize released her and then stepped back from her.

'That should not have happened,' she heard him saying tersely as he turned his back to her. 'It isn't part of our deal.'

Not part of their deal! Chagrin, discomfort, shame and angry humiliation—Petra felt them all in an icy shock wave that brought her back to reality.

Stiffly she headed for the fax machine, more to give herself something to do than because she was anxious to read its message. When she eventually managed to get her gaze to bring it into focus properly, through the turbulence of her thoughts, it turned out to be merely a flyer from a local tour company, highlighting one of their special offers.

As she focused on the wavering print, willing herself not to turn round and look at Blaize, she heard the door to her suite quietly open and then close again.

Even though she continued to focus on her fax message Petra knew just from the feel of the air around her that Blaize had left.

Some time…one day, maybe…she would be glad that this had happened, she told herself fiercely. She would be glad that they had been interrupted and that he had left her! One day. But not now!

CHAPTER FIVE

MISERABLY Petra pushed her uneaten breakfast away and focused determinedly on the brilliantly sunlit scene beyond the windows of the hotel's breakfast room.

She had decided to eat here this morning rather than on her own in her room, primarily because she had hoped that the busyness of having other people around her would take her mind off the events of the previous evening—and Blaize.

Blaize! Every time she thought about him—which was far, far too often for her own peace of mind, she was swamped by opposing feelings of longing and angry self-contempt, plus a sense of bewilderment and disbelief that she could have ever got herself in such a situation. How could she possibly want him?

Petra frowned as she glanced from the informal breakfast dining area into the hotel foyer, which this morning seemed to be filled with far more uniformed and slightly on edge-looking members of staff than she could remember seeing there before.

The waiter had come to clear away her virtually untouched breakfast, and to spend time before going to meet her aunt Petra walked over to study the board outside a small private office, advertising the trips organised by the hotel. One in particular caught her eye, and she read the details of it a second and then a third time.

An escorted drive into the desert, plus an overnight stay at an exclusive oasis resort where it was possible to experience the wonder and majesty of the desert at first hand!

The desert... Quickly, before she could change her mind, Petra went into the office, emerging ten minutes later having made herself a booking. A full night away from Blaize should surely give her time to assess the damage her physical reaction to him was having on her moral beliefs and get herself back in balance again—give her some 'time out'.

As she walked towards the foyer a subtle voice whispered inside her head that there was an even more reckless and dangerous way of stopping a conflagration in its tracks: namely fighting fire with fire. But by using what? Her own sexual need to destroy itself? As in not just giving in to it but actively encouraging it, fanning it into an inferno that would turn and destroy itself?

There was just enough time for her to go to her suite and tidy up before meeting her aunt. Petra smiled at the nervous-looking group of uniformed staff hovering close to the private lift that went to the penthouse suite.

'Everyone looks very busy today,' she commented.

One of the uniformed men rolled his eyes and explained in a semi-hushed whisper. 'There is a meeting upstairs of the hotel owners.'

The hotel owners. Petra's heart did a nervous little shimmy. Did that mean that Rashid had returned? And if he had how long would it be before he sought her out?

'Mmm...it smells heavenly,' Petra acknowledged with a smile as she sniffed the golden nugget of frankincense her aunt was holding out to her. They were in the spice market, where her aunt had haggled determinedly and very professionally for some spices before picking up the frankincense and offering it to Petra to smell. A little wonderingly now, Petra studied the nugget in her hand.

There was something really awesome about standing

here in the new millennium handling something which had been familiar to people from civilisations so ancient it was barely possible to comprehend the time that separated them. There was something about this land that did that to a person, Petra recognised as she handed the nugget back to the robed vendor, nodding her head in agreement as her aunt suggested a cooling glass of pressed fruit juice.

'I have some good news for you.'

Petra saw that her aunt was beaming, as she handed Petra her drink.

'Your grandfather is feeling much better and he has asked me to invite you to visit him this afternoon.'

Petra almost spilled her drink. Was it merely a coincidence that her grandfather should invite her to visit him at the same time as Sheikh Rashid had returned to Zuran? Her body stiffened defensively.

'I'm sorry, but I'm afraid that won't be possible. I...I have other plans.' Petra was proud of the way she managed to keep her voice so calm and cool, even though she was unable to either meet her aunt's eyes or prevent herself from turning her glass round and round in her hands.

She could sense from the quality of silence that her response was not the one her aunt had been expecting, and immediately she felt guilty and uncomfortable. The last thing she wanted to do was upset or offend her aunt, who had been unstintingly kind to her—but she knew just what her grandfather's real plans for her were, Petra firmly reminded herself.

Her aunt was smiling, but Petra could see that her smile was a little strained.

'Your grandfather will be disappointed, Petra,' her aunt told her quietly. 'He has been looking forward to meeting you, but of course if you are busy...'

'I...I have arranged to take a trip into the desert tomorrow,' Petra heard herself explaining, almost defensively, 'and there are things I need to do beforehand…'

A little gravely her aunt inclined her head in acknowledgement of Petra's explanation.

Her aunt insisted on accompanying Petra back to her hotel, but once there refused Petra's suggestion of a cup of coffee.

Her aunt was on the verge of stepping into the taxi the concierge had summoned for her when, on some instinct she couldn't begin to understand, Petra suddenly hurried after her, telling her huskily, 'I've changed my mind. I…I will come and see my grandfather…'

Petra sank her teeth into her bottom lip, mortified by her own weakness as her aunt beamed her approval and gave her a warm hug.

'I know this cannot be easy for you, Petra, but I promise you your grandfather is not an ogre. He has your best interests at heart.'

A tiny little trickle of warning ran down Petra's spine as she absorbed her aunt's unwittingly ominous words. But it was too late for her to recall her change of mind now.

'Your grandfather rests after lunch, but I shall arrange for a car to collect you and bring you to the villa to see him. The driver will pick you up here at four thirty, if that is convenient?'

There was nothing Petra could do other than nod her head.

She had been half expecting that Blaize would try to make contact with her—after all she had as yet still not paid him anything for his services—but there were no messages waiting for her, and no Blaize either!

Petra tried to tell herself that the lurching sensation inside her chest was simply because she was anxious to discuss the day's developments with him—on a purely business basis, of course—and to determine what course of action should follow. It was only natural, surely, that she should feel both anxiety and a sense of urgency now that Sheikh Rashid had returned. And as for last night—well, what was a kiss, after all? If she had blown both it and her reaction to it a little out of proportion, only she knew it! She wasn't so naïve as to deceive herself that kissing her had meant anything special to Blaize.

So why hadn't he been in touch with her? And why hadn't she insisted on him furnishing her with a means of getting in touch with him?

It was gone two o'clock, but despite the fact that she had not been able to eat her breakfast she did not feel hungry. Her stomach was churning in apprehensive anticipation of her coming meeting with her grandfather, and her tension was turned up an unpleasant few notches by the added anxiety of Rashid's return and the lack of contact from Blaize.

It was time for her to get changed, ready for her meeting with her grandfather. Petra hesitated as she surveyed the contents of her wardrobe. The linen dress and jacket would be a good choice, modest but smart, or perhaps the cool chambray…or… Her hand trembled slightly as she removed a plain dark trouser suit from the cupboard. Simply cut in, a matt black fabric it was an outfit that would always be very special to her. It was the suit her mother had bought her just weeks before her death—a good luck present to Petra for her pre-university interviews.

Instead of wearing it for her interviews, Petra had actually worn it for her parents' funeral. But whenever she touched the soft fabric it wasn't that bleak, shocking day she remembered, but the teasing love in her mother's eyes as she had marched her into the boutique and told her that she was going to buy her a present—the happiness and pride in her smile as she'd insisted that Petra parade in front of her in virtually every suit in the shop before she had finally decreed that this particular one was the right one.

This suit held her very last physical memory of her mother's touch and her mother's love, and sometimes Petra would almost swear she could even smell her mother's scent on it—not the rich Eastern perfume that had always been so much a part of her, but *her* scent, her essence.

Sharp tears pricked Petra's eyes. Her mother might not be here with her now, but in wearing this suit Petra somehow felt that she was taking a part of her at least with her—that they were both together, confronting the man who had caused her so much pain.

The suit still fitted, and in fact if anything was perhaps slightly loose on her, Petra acknowledged as she studied her reflection in the mirror.

It was almost half past four. Time to go down to the foyer.

Her business-like appearance attracted several discreet looks as she made her way to the exit. Once again a red carpet was very much in evidence, leading to where several huge shiny black limousines were waiting, flags flying.

Petra studied them with discreet curiosity as she waited for her own transport to arrive, but her interest in the limousines and their potential occupants was forgotten as a sleek saloon car pulled up in front of her and her cousin Saud got out of the front passenger seat, grinning from ear to ear as he hurried towards her.

As she hugged him, Petra was vaguely aware of a sudden stir amongst the limousine chauffeurs, and the emergence of a group of immaculately robed men from the private entrance. But it was Saud who stopped to gaze at the group, grabbing hold of her arm as he told her in an excited voice, 'There's Rashid—with his great-uncle.'

'What? Where?' Her heartbeat had gone into overdrive, but as Petra craned her neck to look in the direction Saud was pointing the last of the robed men was already getting into the waiting limousine.

'Have you met him yet?' Saud demanded as the cars pulled away 'He's cool, isn't he…?'

Petra suppressed her grim look. It was becoming plain to her that her young cousin hero-worshipped her proposed suitor.

'No, I haven't,' she answered him, getting into the waiting car. But as they drove away from the hotel a sudden thought struck her. 'So, was Rashid wearing robes?'

'Yes that's right,' Saud confirmed.

'Despite his Western upbringing?'

Saud looked baffled. 'Yes,' he agreed, then smiled. 'Oh, I see! Rashid's father and his uncle—who is a member of our Royal Family—were very, very close. Rashid's great-uncle has acted as a…a sponsor to Rashid since his parents' death—they were killed when their plane crashed in the desert. I do not remember, since I was not even born then and Rashid himself was only young, but I have heard my father and my grandfather talk of it. Rashid was away in England at the time, at school, but his great-uncle welcomed him into his own family as though Rashid were his son. It is a great honour to our family that his great-uncle favours Rashid's marriage to you. It is just as well that you are a modest woman though, cousin, because Rashid does not approve of the behaviour of some of the tourists who come here to Zuran,' Saud told her.

'Oh, doesn't he?' She demanded with dangerous softness. 'And what about his own behaviour? Is that—'

'Rashid is a very moral man—everyone who knows him knows that. He has very strong values. Zara, my friend and second cousin, says that she feels embarrassed for her own sex when she sees the way that women pursue him. He is very rich, you know, and when they come to the hotel complex and see him they try to attract his attention. But he is not interested in them. Zara says that this is because…' He paused with a self-conscious look in Petra's direction, but she was too infuriated by his naïve revelations to pay much attention.

'Rashid is a very proud man and he would never permit himself or anyone connected with him to do anything to damage the name of his family,' Saud continued solemnly.

At any other time Saud's youthful fervour and seriousness would have brought an amused and tender smile to Petra's lips, but right now his innocent declaration had really got her back up and reinforced her fast-growing animosity to this as yet unmet man, who had patronisingly deigned to consider her as a potential wife.

Well, he was going to discover in no uncertain terms, and hopefully very soon, that she was exactly the type of woman he most despised!

In fact, Petra reflected grimly, the more she heard about Sheikh Rashid the more she knew that there was no way she could ever want to marry him!

They had reached the family villa now, and Petra held her breath a little as they drove through the almost fortress-like entrance into the courtyard that lay beyond it.

Her grandfather insisted on remaining in what had been the family's original home when Zuran had been a trading port and the family rich merchants—although, as her aunt had explained to her, in recent years Petra's uncle had persuaded him to add a large modern extension to the villa. In this older part, though, traditional wind towers still decorated the roofline.

The family no longer adopted the traditional custom of separate living quarters for women, as Petra's mother had told her had been the case when she was a girl, but her aunt quickly explained to Petra, once she had been ushered inside to a cool, elegantly furnished salon, that her grandfather still preferred to keep his own private quarters.

'Kahrun, his manservant, will take you to him,' her aunt informed her. 'He has been very ill, Petra,' she continued hesitantly, 'and I would ask that you…make allowances for…for his ways, even though they are not your own. He loved your mother very much, and her death…' She paused and shook her head whilst Petra forced herself to bite back on her instinctive fierce need to question what her aunt was saying.

A maid arrived with a welcome drink of strong fragrant coffee. Her mother had never lost her love of the drink, and just to smell it reminded Petra so much of her.

Several minutes later, when Petra had refused a second cup, a soft-footed servant arrived and bowed to her, before indicating that she was to follow him.

Her heart thudding but her head held high, Petra did so. They seemed to traverse a maze of corridors before he finally paused outside a heavily carved pair of wooden doors.

The room beyond them was cool and shadowy, its narrow windows overlooking an enclosed garden from which Petra could hear the sound of water so beloved by desert people. The air inside the room smelled of spices—the frankincense she had breathed in this morning, and sandalwood, bringing back to her vivid memories of the small box in which her mother had kept her most precious memories of her lost home and family.

As her emotions momentarily blurred her vision it was impossible for Petra to fully make out the features of the man reclining on the divan several feet away from her.

She could hear him, though, as he commanded, 'Come closer to me so that I may see you. My doctor has forbidden me to overtire myself and so I must lie on this wretched divan on pain of incurring his displeasure.'

Petra heard the small snort of derisive laughter that accompanied the complaint as she blinked away her emotional reaction.

Her mother had described her father in terms that had conjured up for Petra a mental vision of a man who was cruelly strong and stubborn—a man who had overwhelmed and overpowered her mother emotionally—and now that her vision was clearing she had expected to see all those things reflected in him now. But the man in front of her looked unexpectedly frail. One long-fingered hand lay on top of the richly embroidered coverlet, and Petra could see in his profile the pride her mother had described to her so often. But in the dark eyes whose scrutiny seemed to search her face with avid hunger she could see nothing of the rejection and anger that had hurt her mother so badly.

'I don't look very much like my mother,' Petra told him coolly.

'You do not need to look like her. You are of her, and that is enough. Child of my child! Blood of my blood! I have waited a very long time for you to come here to me, Petra. Sometimes I have feared that you would not come in time, and that I would never know you with my outer senses. Although I have always known you with my heart. You are wrong,' he added abruptly, his voice suddenly stronger. 'You are very like my Mija. She was the child of my heart—my youngest child. Her mother was my third wife.'

Angrily Petra looked away.

'You do not approve. No, do not deny it—I can see it in your eyes. How they flash and burn with your emotions! In that too you are like your mother.'

Petra couldn't trust herself to speak.

It had shocked her, though, to realise how frail he looked. She had known that he would be old—he had been in his forties when her mother had been born—but somehow she had convinced herself that he would still be the strong, fierce man her mother had remembered from her own child-hood. Not this obviously elderly white-bearded person whose dark eyes seemed to hold a mixture of compassion and understanding that unsettled her.

Somehow the curt words she had intended to speak to him, the demands she had planned to make to know just why he had wanted to see her, the cynicism and contempt she had planned to let him see, refused to be summoned.

Instead…instead…

As she lifted her hand the gold bangle caught the light. Immediately her grandfather stiffened.

'You are wearing Mija's bracelet,' he whispered. 'It was my last gift to her… I have a photograph of her here, wear-ing it.'

To Petra's astonishment he reached out and picked up a heavy photograph album which Petra hadn't previously no-ticed, beckoning her to come closer so that she could see what he wanted to show her.

As his frail fingers lifted the pages Petra felt her heart turn over. Every photograph in the book was of her mother, and some of them…

She could feel her eyes starting to burn with tears as she recognised one of them. It was a photograph of herself as a very new baby with her mother. Her father had had ex-actly the same picture on his desk, in the room which had been his office when he'd worked at home!

Immediately she put out her hand to stop him from turn-ing any more of the pages, unable to stop herself from demanding in a shaky voice, 'That photograph—how…?'

'Your father sent it to me,' he told her. 'He sent me many photographs of you, Petra, and many letters, too.'

'My father!' This was news to Petra, and it took her several minutes to absorb it properly. It was hard enough to accept that her father could have done such a thing, but what was even harder was knowing that he had kept his actions a secret from her. And from her mother? Petra felt cold. Surely not? What could have motivated him when he had known how badly her mother had been hurt by her father's actions?

As her glance met that of her grandfather Petra knew that he could see what she was thinking.

A little awkwardly he beckoned her to move closer to him. When she hesitated, he told her, 'There is a box, over there. I would like you to bring it to me.'

The box in question was sitting on an intricately carved table, its surface smooth and warm to Petra's touch. She could tell just by looking at it that it was very old.

'This belonged to my own grandfather,' her grandfather said as she took it to him.

'He was a merchant and this box went everywhere with him. He said that it had originally been made for one of the sultans of the great Ottoman Empire.' He gave a small smile. 'He was a great story-teller, and many times as a small child I would neglect my lessons to sit at his feet and listen to his tales. Whether they were true or not!'

As he was speaking he was reaching for a heavy bunch of keys, searching through them until he found the one he was looking for.

His fingers, obviously stiffened by old age, struggled to insert the key in the tiny lock and then turn it, but once he had done so and pushed back the lid Petra was aware of the mingled scents of sandalwood and age that rose from its interior.

She couldn't see what was inside the box, but waited patiently as her grandfather sighed and muttered to himself, obviously sifting through its contents until he had finally found what he wanted.

'Read this,' he commanded her brusquely, handing her a worn airmail envelope.

'It is your father's letter to me, telling me of your birth.'

Hesitantly Petra took the envelope from him. She wasn't sure she was ready to read what her father might have written. All her life she had looked up to him as a man of strong sturdy morals and infinite compassion, a man of the highest probity and honour. If she should read something that damaged that belief...

'Read,' her grandfather was urging her impatiently.

Taking a deep breath, Petra did so.

The letter was addressed to her grandfather with true diplomatic formality, using his titles.

'To he who is the father of my beloved wife Mija,

I have the felicitation of informing you that I am now the proud father of the most beautiful baby daughter. I had thought when Mija came into my life that there could be no place in it to love another human being, so great and all-encompassing is my love for her, but I was wrong. I write to you now as one father to another to tell you of the most wonderful, precious gift we have received in Petra's birth, and to tell you also that we now share common ground—we are both fathers—we have both been granted the unique privilege of being gifted with daughters.

And it is as a father that I write to you begging you to reconsider your decision regarding the exclusion of Mija from your family—for your own sake and not ours. I have made a solemn vow that I shall surround Mija

with all the love she will ever need. We have each other
and our beautiful daughter and our lives will be filled
with love and joy. But what of you? You have turned
away your own daughter and denied yourself her love
and that of the grandchild she has given you.

I beg you to think of this and to put aside your pride.
I know how much it would mean to Mija to have word
from you, especially at this time.

Whatever your decision, I have made a vow to my
daughter that I shall ensure that you, her grandfather, and
the rest of the family are kept informed of her life.

The letter bore her father's formal signature at its end,
but Petra could barely focus on it as the paper trembled in
her hand and her eyes stung with tears. It shamed her that
she could have doubted her father for so much as a single
heartbeat.

As he took the letter from her, returning it to its envelope
and replacing it carefully in the box before relocking it, her
grandfather said gruffly, 'Your father was a good man, even
though he was not the man I would have chosen for my
Mija.'

'My father was a wonderful, wonderful, very special
man,' Petra corrected him proudly.

Had her mother known what her father had done? If so
she had never spoken of it to her, but then neither had her
father! Suddenly, despite her private knowledge of her
grandfather's secret purpose in wanting her here in Zuran,
she was glad that she had come!

'He understood my feelings as a father,' her grandfather
acknowledged.

Petra had to close her eyes to conceal the intensity of
the emotions that rushed over her.

'You say that now! You claim to have loved my mother.

But you never made any attempt to contact her—to…'
Petra refused to say the word 'forgive', because so far as
she was concerned her mother was the one who had the
right to extend that largesse, not her grandfather! 'You must
have known how much it would have meant to her to hear
from you!'

Impossible for her to hold back her feelings—or her
pain—any longer. Petra knew that her grandfather must be
able to hear it in her voice just as she could herself.

'When she left you told her that you would never permit
her name to be spoken in your hearing ever again. You said
that she was dead to you and to her family, and you forbade
them to have anything to do with her. You let her die—'

Petra heard herself sobbing like a lost child. 'You let her
die believing that you had stopped loving her! How could
you do that?'

As Petra fought for self-control she could see the pain
shadowing her grandfather's eyes, and suddenly it seemed
as though he shrunk a little, and looked even older and
more fragile than he had done when she had first walked
into the room.

'There is nothing I can say that will ease your pain. No
words I can offer you will lighten either your burden—or
my own,' she heard him saying sombrely. 'It is still too
soon. Perhaps in time… But at my age time is no longer
either a friend or an ally. I am sorry that we have not been
able to make you properly welcome here in your mother's
home, Petra, but now that that old fool my doctor has
ceased his unnecessary fussing I shall give instructions that
a room is to be prepared for you. We have much to discuss
together, you and I.'

Like his desire to see her married to the man of his
choice? Petra wondered suspiciously, abruptly back on her
guard; he might look frail and sorrowful now, but she

couldn't forget the cunning and deceit which history had already proved him capable of.

And once she was living here beneath his roof she would virtually be a prisoner. With no passport she had no means of leaving the country! Which meant it was imperative that she persisted with her plan to have Rashid refuse to consider her as a wife.

Even if that meant seeing Blaize again and the risk that could entail?

Unable to give herself a truly rational answer, Petra diverted her own thoughts by telling her grandfather, in a cool voice she intended would make him fully aware of her determination to retain her independence, 'I have made arrangements for an overnight trip into the desert tomorrow, so—'

'The desert!' To her surprise, his eyes lit up with pleasure and approval. 'It is good that you wish to see the land that is so much a part of your heritage. I wish that it was possible for me to go with you! But you shall tell me all about it! I shall inform your hotel that Kahrun will be collecting you to bring you here once you return.'

He was beginning to look tired, but instinctively Petra sensed that his pride would not allow him to admit any weakness. Whatever else she had been lied to about, Petra could see now that so far as his health was concerned he had genuinely been ill. It was there in the greyish tinge to his skin, the vulnerability of his frail frame. An unexpected—and unwanted—emotion filled her: a sense of kinship and closeness, an awareness of the blood tie they shared that she simply had not been prepared for and which it seemed she had no weapons to fight against. He was her grandfather, the man who had given life to the mother she had loved so much, a potential bridge via which she could recapture and relive some of her most precious memories.

Swallowing against the lump in her throat, Petra got up, and as her grandfather reached out his hands to her, Petra placed hers in them.

'Beloved child of my beloved child,' he whispered brokenly to her, and then the door opened and Kahrun, his manservant, arrived to escort her back to the hotel.

It was only when she was finally being driven back to her hotel by Kahrun that Petra mentally questioned just why she had not challenged her grandfather with her knowledge of his plans for her. Had the emotions he had displayed been genuine and as overwhelming as they had seemed? Or had he simply been manipulating the situation and her for his own ends? Surely she wasn't foolish enough to be influenced by her own unwilling acknowledgement of his frailty, a long-ago letter from her father, and a few emotional words?

But there was more to the situation than that! A lot more! In his presence, in the home which had once been her mother's, Petra had abruptly been forced to recognise and acknowledge a deep subterranean pool of previously hidden emotions.

Her parents' deaths had forced her to grow up very quickly, to become mature whilst she was still very young, and in many ways had forced her to become her own parent. Her godfather, kind though he was, was a bachelor, a man dedicated to his career, who had had no real idea of the emotional needs of a seventeen-year-old girl. Had she been a different person, Petra knew, she might quite easily have gone off the rails. Her godfather's lifestyle meant that she had been allowed a considerable amount of unsupervised freedom, and she had been called upon to make decisions about her life and her future that should more properly have been made by someone far more adult. The result of this had been that she'd had to 'police' her own behaviour, and to take responsibility for herself, emotionally and morally.

Now, today, in her grandfather's room, she had suddenly realised just what a heavy burden those responsibilities had been, and how much she had yearned to have someone of her own to carry them for her—to counsel and guide her, to protect her, to love her! How much, in fact, she had needed the family which had been denied to her! And how much a small, weak part of her still did...

That was where her real danger lay, she recognised. It lay in her wanting the approval and acceptance of her 'family' so much that she could fall into the trap of allowing herself to exchange her freedom and independence for them!

The weight of her own thoughts was beginning to make her head ache.

CHAPTER SIX

GRIMLY Petra blinked the slight grittiness from her eyes as she studied her reflection in her bedroom mirror. She had barely slept, and when she had she had been tormented by confusing dark-edged dreams in which she was being pursued by a white-robed persecutor, his features hidden from her. In her nightmare she had called out to Blaize to rescue her, but although she could see him he had not been paying any heed to her pleas, had instead been engrossed with the scantily clad bevy of women surrounding him.

Only once had he actually turned to look at her, and then he had shaken his head and told her cruelly, 'Go away, little virgin. I do not want you.'

And now, even though the night was over, Petra felt as though its dark shadow still hung over her. There was hardly any time left for her to convince Rashid that she was not a suitable bride, and once again Blaize had made no attempt to get in touch with her.

Lethargically she moved away from the mirror. She had already packed an overnight bag, as instructed by the fax she had received from the tour operator, and she was dressed in what she hoped would be a suitable outfit of short-sleeved tee shirt and a pair of khaki combat-style pants with sturdy and hopefully sand-proof trainers. She had, as instructed, a long-sleeved top to cover her arms from the heat and the sand, a hat, a pair of sunglasses and a large bottle of water. But the sense of adventure and intrigue with which she had originally booked the trip had gone, leaving in its place a lacklustre feeling of emptiness.

Because she hadn't heard from Blaize? A man she had known less than a week? A man who quite patently cynically used his sexuality to fund a lifestyle that was in direct opposition to everything that Petra herself believed in! She couldn't possibly really be trying to tell herself that she was emotionally attracted to him? That in such a short space of time he had become so necessary to her that a mere twenty-four hours without him had left her feeling that her whole life was empty and worthless?

Now she was afraid, Petra admitted shakily, and with good reason! What she was thinking truly was cause for the horrified chills running down her spine! There was no way she could allow herself to be in love with Blaize.

Be in love? Since when had love entered the equation? she tried to mock herself.

Only two days ago she had been finding it hard to admit that she just might find him sexually attractive. Two days before that she had barely known that he existed. Yet here she was, trying to talk herself into believing she loved him! No, not trying to talk herself into it, trying to talk herself *out* of it, Petra corrected herself swiftly.

Her telephone rang. Quickly she picked up the receiver. It was the front desk informing her that her transport had arrived.

Picking up her overnight bag, Petra told herself sternly that a little breathing space would do her good. What a pity she was living in the modern century, though, and not a previous one where it might have been possible for a traveller attached to a camel train to pass through a country's borders without the necessity of producing a passport...

A group of newly arrived holidaymakers were filling the foyer, and the concierge staff had no time to do anything more than point Petra in the direction of the waiting vehicle she could see outside, a logo painted on its side.

Even with her sunglasses the sunlight was so strong that she was momentarily blinded as she headed for the four-wheel drive vehicle, and it was whilst she was still trying to accustom her eyes to the brilliance that she felt strong hands relieve her of her overnight bag, and then grasp her waist to help her into the front passenger seat of the vehicle.

She heard the slam of the passenger door, and then the closing rear door. As her driver climbed into the driving seat she turned her head to look at him, her eyes widening in shock as she realised just who her driver was!

'Blaize!' she exclaimed weakly. 'What are you doing here?'

Petra tried to drag her gaze away from him as she gulped in air. Her chest had gone so tight it hurt, and she could feel the heat surging through her body as it reacted with telltale swiftness to his presence.

'You booked a trip into the desert,' he told her laconically as he set the vehicle in motion and drove off.

'Yes... But...'

'But what?' he challenged her with an almost bored shrug. 'I thought it made more sense for me to take you. The desert can be a very seductive place, so I've been told, and your intended isn't going to like knowing that his bride-to-be has spent the night in the desert with another man. How did you get on with your grandfather? Is all forgiven?' he asked her flippantly.

'My mother is the one who is owed forgiveness,' Petra told him quietly. 'And she died believing that he had stopped loving her.'

There was a small silence before Blaize responded in a voice that sounded unfamiliarly serious.

'Then I imagine that your grandfather will find it extremely difficult to forgive himself.'

'His feelings are of no concern to me!' Petra told Blaize.

angrily, and then stopped speaking as an inner voice told her that she was not being entirely truthful. 'I thought that he was pretending to be ill,' she heard herself telling Blaize.

'And was he?' he asked.

'No,' Petra acknowledged. 'But that still does not mean he has the right to do what he is trying to do to me—use me for his own selfish ends.'

'Perhaps he thinks this marriage will be beneficial for you,' Blaize suggested. 'His generation still believe that a woman needs a protector, a husband, and it would keep you here, close to your mother's family, and provide for you financially.'

'What?' Petra stared at him in disbelief. 'How can you say that after what I have told you? My feelings…my needs…are the last thing he is thinking about.'

'You mean *you* believe they are! If you were to leave Zuran now, what would you do…where would you go?'

Petra glared at him. Why was he suddenly trying to play the devil's advocate? For amusement?

'I would go home…to the UK. I'm twenty-three, and although I have a good degree I would like to get my Master's. There's so much social inequality in the world that needs addressing—working in the field for the aid agency showed me that. I would like to do something to help other people.'

'As a rich man's wife you could do far more than as a mere fieldworker.'

'I've already told you—I could never marry a man I did not love and respect. And from what Saud has told me it sounds as though I would be expected to treat Rashid as though he's a minor god! Saud hero-worships him, and can't wait for me to marry him so that he can officially claim Rashid as a relative. And of course he isn't the only one! From the sound of it, my whole family are delirious with joy at the prospect of this marriage. All I seem to hear is ''Rashid this'' and ''Rashid that''…'

'Your cousin seems to be a positive wealth of information about the man.'

There was a certain dryness in Blaize's voice that made Petra frown a little. 'Saud is young and impressionable. Like I said, he obviously hero-worships Rashid, and thinks he can do no wrong.'

'A young person sometimes benefits from a role model and mentor.'

'Oh, I agree. But if a man who quite plainly divides women into two separate groups—good and bad, moral and immoral—whilst no doubt maintaining for himself the right to live exactly as he chooses, is not, in my opinion, a good role model—'

'If you look to your left now, you might just catch a glimpse of the royal horses being exercised,' Blaize interrupted her calmly.

Stopped in mid-tirade, Petra was tempted to continue with her diatribe—but then she saw the horses and their jockeys, and the sheer thrill of seeing so much power and beauty kept her silent as she inwardly paid homage to the spectacle they created.

'You are still totally opposed to this marriage, then, I take it?' Blaize asked her several minutes later.

'Of course. How could I not be? I can't marry a man I don't love.'

'You might find you could come to love him after the marriage.'

Petra gave him a scornful look.

'Never,' she denied vehemently. 'And anyway even if I did, I somehow doubt that the Sheikh is likely to return my feelings. No, all our marriage would mean to him would be the successful conclusion to a diplomatic arrangement.

I've got to make him change his mind and refuse to even countenance the idea.'

'Have you thought that he may feel the same way about this situation as you do yourself? Have you thought of contacting him and perhaps discussing things with him?'

Petra gave him a withering look.

'Unlike me, he has had the chance to refuse to become involved! After all, without his tacit acceptance the whole situation could simply not exist. Anyway, why are you suddenly so keen to promote him? Don't you want to earn five thousand pounds any more?' she demanded.

Or was it perhaps that he wanted her out of his life because he had sensed how she felt about him? A man like him would quite definitely not want the complications of having a woman fall in love with him!

Fall in love? But she hadn't done that, had she? Petra closed her eyes in helpless self-anger. Hadn't she got enough unwanted emotional pain to carry through life as excess baggage already, without deliberately inviting more?

'Hang on tight. We'll be leaving the highway soon and going into true desert terrain,' Blaize warned her, without taking his eyes off the road.

Petra gasped and clung to her seat as they veered off the road and crested the first of a series of sand dunes, following what to her was a barely discernible track—although Blaize did not seem to be having any trouble in finding and following it.

Within minutes it seemed to Petra the road had vanished and the landscape had become a vast expanse of sand dunes, stretching from horizon to horizon. A little anxiously she swivelled round in her seat, craning her neck to look in the direction they had just come.

'How…how do you know the way?' she asked Blaize a little uncertainly.

'I can tell the direction we are travelling by the position of the sun,' he said with a small dismissive shrug, and then added derisively, 'And besides, these all-terrain vehicles are equipped with navigation systems and a compass. Essential in this type of country. A bad sandstorm can not only reduce visibility to nought, it can also wipe out existing trails. See that over there?' he commanded, pointing in the direction of where a bird was hovering motionless, a mere dot in the hot blue emptiness of the sky.

'What is it?' Petra asked him.

'A hunting falcon,' he told her, reaching into the compartment between them. As he did so his fingertips inadvertently brushed against her knee and immediately her body reacted, pouring a lava hot molten tide of sharp longing through her. Petra could feel her whole body tightening in wanton hunger for him. If she turned to him now, covered his hand with her own, his mouth with her own; if she reached out and touched him as she wanted him to touch her... But it was too late. He had already moved away and was producing a pair of binoculars, which he offered to her. Binoculars! When what she wanted him to offer her was...was himself!

'Take a closer look,' he instructed her. 'It will probably be a trained bird. A number of Zuran's richest inhabitants maintain their own falconries, where birds are reared and trained. It's an ancient craft which is still practised here.'

As Petra watched the bird suddenly turned and wheeled and was quickly out of sight, as though responding to some unseen summons.

'They often have displays of falconry at the desert village where we'll be spending the night,' Blaize informed her. 'Most people find the birds too fearsome to approach, but in actual fact the camels are probably more dangerous.'

'So my mother told me,' Petra replied.

She was finding it a little disconcerting that Blaize, the beach bum, should so suddenly and unexpectedly prove to be so knowledgeable about the local culture and history. Not wanting to be outdone, she was quick to remind him that she was, after all, a part of that culture, even if this was the first time she was experiencing it firsthand.

There was quite definitely a stirring awesomeness about the desert, but Petra was finding it difficult to give her exclusive attention to her surroundings because of the effect that Blaize himself was having on her.

But that did not mean that she had fallen in love with him, she reassured herself fiercely. Just because her heart was beating with an unfamiliar speed, and she dared not look properly at him because when she did she wanted to keep on looking…and do much, much more than just merely look, she admitted breathlessly. But that did not mean…anything. In fact it meant nothing—nothing at all other than that she was physically aware of him.

Aware of him and responsive to him… And surely, if she was truly honest with herself, not just physically…

'You look flushed,' she heard Blaize telling her brusquely. 'You must make sure that you drink plenty of water. The desert is the last place to get dehydrated.'

Perhaps she ought to be glad that he believed her heightened colour was caused by the sun's heat rather than guessing that it was caused by the unwanted sensuality of her own desire for him, Petra reflected inwardly.

She had believed that her mother's reminiscences of her own childhood trips into the desert had prepared her for what she might expect, but Petra still found that she was holding her breath and then expelling it in a sharp sound of excitement as they crested yet another sand dune. There before them, shimmering beneath the sun's heat like a mirage, lay the oasis and the encampment which had been recreated to give tourists like herself a taste of what desert living had been all about in the days when Nomad tribes had still roamed the desert, travelling from one oasis to another.

Several other four-wheel drive vehicles were already parked close to one another and Blaize pulled up next to them.

'Wait here,' Blaize told her. 'I'll go and find out which tent has been assigned to us.'

To *them*? Petra's stomach muscles were quivering with the effort of controlling her emotions when Blaize returned several minutes later and she walked into what was more properly a pavilion than a mere tent, at the farthest edge of the encampment. She discovered that it was divided inside into three completely separate sections, which comprised a living room area, complete with rich, patterned oriental carpets and silk-covered divans, as well as two separated bedrooms. The shower block, Blaize informed her, was more mundanely housed on its own, and provided up-to-the-minute facilities.

Petra was only half listening to him. She had unfastened the doorway leading to one of the bedrooms and was staring in disbelieving delight at its interior.

Unlike her very modern bedroom at the hotel, this really was straight out of an Arabian Nights fantasy.

The interior 'walls' of the pavilion were hung with a rich mixture of embroidered silks in shimmering oriental colours, embellished with gold thread which caught the light from the lamps placed on low, heavily carved chests dotted around the surprisingly spacious room.

The bed itself, whilst only slightly raised off the rug-covered floor, like the walls was covered in beautiful silk throws, and from the ceiling there hung sheer muslin voiles, currently tied back, which Petra suspected would cover the whole bed when untied. The effect was one of unsurpassable opulence and sensuality, and Petra was half afraid to even blink, just in case she discovered that the entire room was merely a mirage.

'Something wrong?' she heard Blaize asking from behind her.

Immediately Petra shook her head.

'No. It's…it's wonderful…'

'Arabian Nights meets MGM,' Blaize pronounced briefly and almost sardonically as he glanced past her into the room.

'It's beautiful.' Petra defended her new temporary home.

'Officially, it's the honeymoon suite,' Blaize informed her drily, adding, 'But don't worry—just in case they don't get any honeymooners—or if they do but they fall out—they keep the other room kitted out as a second bedroom.'

The honeymoon suite! Why had they been given that? Or had Blaize perhaps asked for it deliberately, to reinforce the idea that they were lovers?

'If you want to have a camel ride, now's the time,' Blaize was continuing, patently oblivious to the sensuality and allure of the silk-hung bedroom and the temptation that was affecting Petra so forcibly.

'More coffee?'

Smiling, Petra shook her head, covering her cup with her hand in the traditional gesture that meant that she had had enough.

It was nearly eleven o'clock in the evening, and the dishes had been cleared away following their evening meal, ready for the entertainment to begin.

Petra could feel the excited expectation emanating from the gathered onlookers as the musicians changed beat and out of one of the tents a stunningly beautiful woman shimmied, dressed in a traditional dancing costume, jewels sparkling on her fingers and of course in her navel as she swayed provocatively to the sound of the music. Her body undulated sensuously, her dark eyes flashing smoky temptation above her veil as she rolled her hips, her whole body, and most especially the bare, smooth, taut brown expanse of her belly in rhythmic time to the music.

To one side of her a group of tourists were passing a hubble-bubble pipe between one another, the girls giggling softly as they breathed in the sweet taste of the strawberry-flavoured smoke. Its effect was supposed to be mildly euphoric, and Petra hesitated a little when it was passed on to her.

'If you don't try it you have to pay a forfeit and get up and dance with our belly dancer,' the tour guide with the large party who had just passed her the pipe teased Petra.

Rather than appear standoffish, Petra took a quick breath, relaxing as she smelled the innocuous scent of the strawberries and then offering the pipe to Blaize, only to realise that he had got up and walked away. He was talking to the falconer, who was still holding one of his now hooded birds, the gold tooling on the leather gloves, gleaming in the firelight.

As she handed the pipe back to the waiting tour guide, Petra realised that she wasn't the only woman there looking at Blaize. The belly dancer was focusing her gaze and her openly inviting body movements on him, ignoring the rest of them and turning to face him, moving closer and closer to him.

And as for Blaize…! A sensation of sheer white-hot jealousy knifed through Petra as she saw the way he was watching the dancer and smiling at her.

Petra had believed that she knew pain, but now, shockingly, she realised that all she had experienced was one of its many dimensions. Right now, watching Blaize look at another woman when she ached, yearned, needed to have him look only at her, unlocked for her the door to an agonising new world of pain!

Thoughts, longings, needs hitherto denied and forbidden broke loose from the control she had imposed on them, one after the other, until she was exposed to an entire avalanche of them. They buried for ever any possibility of her denying what her feelings for Blaize really were!

Frantically she struggled to make sense of what was happening. In the eerie pristine silence that followed the inner explosion, her thought processes were frozen.

How was it possible for her to love Blaize? Petra felt as though she had suddenly become one of those small figures in a child's snowstorm ball, who had just had her whole world and all her perceptions of what was in it turned vigorously upside down. But say she had got it wrong. Say she did not really love Blaize. Mentally she tried to imagine how she would feel if she were never to see him again.

The intensity of her pain made her catch her breath. Was this how her mother had felt about her father? It must have been. But things had been different for her mother, Petra had to remind herself. Her mother had known that her love was returned…shared… That she was loved as much as she herself loved.

The music was reaching a crescendo, and Petra shivered as she felt and saw the raw sensuality of the dancer's movements, her passionate determination to make Blaize notice her, choose her. Blaize himself had turned round and was watching her. The girl danced faster and faster, and then as the music exploded in climactic triumph she flung herself bodily as Blaize's feet.

Petra could tell from the reaction of the guides and the

robed men watching that this was not the normal finale to the dance. Instinctively she knew that the girl did not normally offer herself with such sexual blatancy to one of the male onlookers the way she just had done to Blaize, and immediately her own jealousy burned to a white heat.

She wanted to run to the girl and push her away—to tell her that Blaize belonged to her. But of course he did not!

The audience were good-humouredly throwing money onto the floor for the dancer, as they had been encouraged to do, but the dancer remained prostrate in front of Blaize, not acknowledging their generosity. It was left to one of the male fire-eaters who had been entertaining them earlier to pick it up.

As Petra watched Blaize watching the girl she wondered what he was thinking. He said something to one of the men he had been speaking with, who inclined his head as though in deference to Blaize before going over to the girl and bending towards her.

What was the man saying to her? Petra wondered jealously. What message had Blaize given the man to give her? Had he told her that he would see her later? The girl was getting up. She looked at Blaize, a proud, challenging flash of dark eyes, before walking slowly away, her hips swaying provocatively as she did so, her spine straight.

How could any man resist such an invitation? Petra wondered bleakly. Why would a man like Blaize even try to do so? And why, oh, why did a woman like her have to fall in love with him?

The evening was drawing to a close. People were finishing off their drinks and retiring to their pavilions.

Petra looked towards Blaize, who was still talking to the falconer and some other men. The dancer had disappeared, and Blaize was showing no signs of coming over to her or even looking at her.

Tiredly Petra got up and made her own way to their pavilion, collecting her things and then heading for the shower block. Too much was happening to her too quickly. Since arriving in this country she had been forced to confront aspects of herself and her feelings that it was very hard for her to accept.

Suddenly, standing beneath the warm spray of the shower, she longed achingly to be able to turn back the clock and return to a time when she had known nothing of the complexities that meeting her grandfather would bring. A time when she would have laughed out loud in disbelief if anyone had suggested that she would fall in love with a man like Blaize.

The camp was settling down to sleep when she made her way back to her pavilion. The soft glow of the lamps added to the air of mystery and enticement of its interior.

Someone had placed a dish of dates on one of the low carved tables in the sitting area, and silk cushions were placed invitingly on the floor in front of it, but Petra had no stomach for the sweetness of the dates—no stomach for anything, really, she admitted, now that her heart was soured by the anguish of her unreturnable love for Blaize. After all, even if he were by some impossible means to return her feelings, how could there be any future for them?

It wasn't a matter of money. That didn't come into it. Blaize could have had nothing and she would have loved him proudly and joyously. But how could she feel anything other than disquiet and distress at loving a man who used himself in the way that Blaize did? It was that which hurt her more than anything else! Even more than thinking about him with another woman? The belly dancer for instance?

Petra curled her hands into small fists. Where was he now? He was not in his room. The fabric covering the entrance to it was tied back so that she could see that the space beyond was empty.

Unlike hers, the 'walls' of his room were hung with darker, heavier fabric, which if anything was even more richly embroidered in gold than her own. Opulent fur-mimicking throws were heaped on the bed. There was a beautiful rug on the floor and a dish of sweet almond cakes on the table in front of the divan, along with a pot of richly fragrant coffee.

It was a setting fit for an Arabian prince, Petra reflected admiringly. And a retreat to which that same prince could bring the dancing girl of his choice, a dangerous inner voice taunted her.

Quickly Petra suppressed it. Blaize was no prince, Arabian or otherwise, and as for the dancing girl…

But where was he? Virtually the whole camp seemed to have settled down to sleep, and yet there was no sign of him.

Restlessly Petra paced the small pavillioned sitting area, tensing as the opening flap was abruptly pushed back and Blaize came in. He was stripped to the waist, a towel round his shoulders, his hair damp, and as he came in he brought with him the scent of the night and the desert—and of himself.

Petra felt her insides turn softly, compliantly liquid, longing pulsing through her as she gazed helplessly at his body.

She hadn't truly appreciated its magnificence the first time she had seen it, hadn't been able to sense its male capacity for sensuality and female pleasure, but now she could.

Abruptly her eyes narrowed, her gaze focusing on the angry claw-marks on his arm, which were still oozing blood slightly. Immediately the earth rocked beneath her feet and she was savaged by her own jealousy.

He had been with the dancer, and she had clawed her mark of possession on him!

Her mark of passion!

Before she could even recognise what she was doing, never mind stop herself, Petra had clenched her hands into small fists and advanced on him, demanding furiously, 'Where have you been? As if I didn't know! Was she good? Better than the rich tourists who pay you for your favours?'

'What…?'

Like lightning the changing expressions chased one another across his face, frowning disbelief followed by a warning, taut concentration. In its place followed an even more dangerous flash of sheeting anger and his mouth compressed and a tiny nerve pulsed in his jaw.

But Petra was in no mood to heed warning signs, and her eyes glittered with a fury every bit feral as his as she stated sarcastically, 'Silly me! I thought the whole purpose of us being here together was to convince the outside world that *we* are lovers! But obviously I was wrong and it's not! No—what's obviously far more important to you than honouring the arrangement we made is enjoying the…the sexual favours of an…an oversexed belly dancer. But then of course the two of you have something in common, don't you? You both sell your sexual favours for money and—'

Petra gave a small squeak as she was suddenly lifted off her feet. Her arms were in a vice-like grip as Blaize held her so that their eyes were on the same level.

'You should check your facts before you start throwing insults like that around,' he told her, biting the words into small barbed insults, his mouth barely moving as he hurled them lividly at her. 'If you were a man— But you aren't, are you?' he demanded, his voice suddenly changing to a soft sneer as he added, 'You aren't even much of a woman…just an over-excited, over-heated virgin, aching with curiosity to know what it's all about. No, don't deny it. It's written all over you—all over every single one of those big-eyed looks you keep on giving me when you think I don't notice. You're just desperate to find out what sex is, aren't you? Well, I'm sorry to disappoint you, but you just don't have what it takes to encourage me to let you find out!'

Every single word he had uttered had found its mark, and Petra felt as though she was slowly dying from the pain of the wounds he had inflicted. But there was no way she was going to let him see that—no way she was going to stop fighting...

'You mean that I haven't offered you enough money?' she taunted him recklessly.

'Enough money?' To Petra's disbelief, he threw back his head and laughed harshly.

'Despite what you so obviously think, it isn't money that turns me on, Petra, that makes me want a woman, ache for her so I can't rest until I possess her in every way there is. Until I wake up with her beside me in the morning, knowing that her body still wears my touch, inside and out, that she is so much a part of me that she still smells of me. But you don't know anything about that, do you? You know nothing about a man's desire...the compulsion that drives him to want a woman. Shall I show you? Is that what you want?'

Petra knew that she ought to deny what he was saying...refuse what he was offering her. But all she could do was let her gaze cling helplessly to his, her body motionless in his arms as he lowered his head towards hers!

As his lips touched hers she made a tiny almost mute sound at the back of her throat. Now she knew what it was like to be driven by a need, a thirst so all-consuming that it burned the soul as well as the body—to crave something, someone, to the point where the pain of that craving was an eternal torment. No Nomad lost in the desert could crave water with anything like the same intensity as she craved Blaize right now!

She moaned as he kissed her, wrapping her arms as tightly around him as she could, savouring the hot, deep thrust of his tongue and pressing close to him.

She could feel the anger pulsing through his body, but she was beyond caring which emotion drove him just so long as he never, ever lifted his mouth from her own.

And then, before she could stop him, he was wresting his mouth from hers, telling her savagely, 'Why the hell am I doing this? I must be going crazy! The last thing I need—or want—right now is—' He had stopped speaking to shake his head, but Petra could guess what he was thinking! What he had been about to say!

The last thing he needed—or wanted—was her!

Driven by the pain of his abrupt rejection of her, held deep in the grip of a primitive urge, an emotional, immediate reaction to his cruel taunting words she couldn't control, Petra lashed out at him, her hand raised.

And when, more by accident than anything, her hand hit the side of his jaw his own shock was mirrored by the expression in her eyes as they rounded and darkened. She shuddered convulsively, as though he had been the one to hit her.

She felt him release her and her feet hit the ground. She knew she must have moved, because suddenly she was in her own bedroom, lying curled up in the centre of the lavish bed whilst her whole body trembled with shock and pain, but she had no awareness of having got there—no awareness of anything since that awful moment when she had felt as well as heard the crack of her open palm against his skin.

How could she have done such a thing? She was totally opposed to all forms of violence. It disgusted her to the point where she felt physically sick that she had acted in such a way, but her dry aching eyes refused to provide her with the comfort of cleansing tears to wash away her guilt.

CHAPTER SEVEN

PAINFULLY Petra stared into the emptiness surrounding her. It was barely twenty minutes or so since Blaize had left her, but to Petra each one of those minutes had felt like an hour as she fought to come to terms with the shock of her own uncharacteristic behaviour. She was being tormented—not just by her unwanted love for Blaize, but by her guilt at the way she had behaved as well.

No matter how righteous her cause or how much provocation she believed she had been made to suffer, she still could not excuse or forgive herself for what she had done. To have been so driven by her own demons that she had resorted to physical violence! A shudder of self-loathing and moral outrage gripped her body.

According to the code by which she had been brought up by her parents, she owed Blaize an apology. Never mind that his own behaviour was open to question—his behaviour was something she was not responsible for. Her own was a different matter.

Apologise to him? After what he had said? After what he had done? After the way he had inflamed her senses, her body, until she had ached so feverishly for him that her longing overwhelmed everything else and then rejected her! Never, never. Never, not even on pain of torture, Petra swore dramatically to herself.

But five minutes later, with her conscience digging into her painfully, refusing to be ignored no matter how tightly she cocooned herself in her righteous indignation and tried to smother its nagging little voice, Petra finally gave in. If she waited too much longer she would be disturbing Blaize in the middle of his night's sleep!

Nervously, she reached for her robe and took a deep breath.

In the outer room the oil lamps had burned low, casting soft long shadows against the darkness.

Surely her apology could wait until morning? a craven little voice urged her. Blaize might well already be asleep. But Petra refused to allow herself to listen to it. She had done something wrong and now she must make amends!

Taking a deep breath, Petra lifted back the entrance fabric to Blaize's bedroom. In the few seconds it took her eyes to adjust to the darkness she could hear the noisy, anxious slam of her own heart against her ribs, and instinctively she placed one hand against it, as though trying to silence it.

The full moon outside lifted the darkness just enough for her to be able to make out Blaize's sleeping form beneath the bedcovers. He was lying on his side, with his face towards her, but turned into the pillow so that she could not tell whether he was awake or not. Tentatively she whispered his name, but there was no response. Was he asleep?

If she left now he would never even know she had been here. Longingly she looked back towards the exit, but the stubborn pride her father had always teased her about, that she had inherited from her grandfather, refused to allow her to make a craven escape without first checking that he was actually sleeping.

Head held high, she walked over to the bed. Like her own it was easily wide enough for two people. Uncertainly she looked at Blaize. Was he asleep? He certainly wasn't moving. Quietly she crept a little closer, automatically balancing one knee on the bed as she did so in order to get a closer look at him.

Tentatively she whispered his name. If he didn't respond

and was asleep then she could return to her own bed with a clear conscience and save her apology until the morning, knowing that she had at least tried to deliver it!

He hadn't uttered a sound. Exhaling softly in relief, Petra started to back away—and then froze as with shocking speed he reached out and gripped her wrist, demanding tauntingly, 'Sleepwalking Petra?'

His fingers burned against her skin, and as though he had guessed his thumb probed the uncoordinated thud of her pulse as though he was monitoring her reaction to him.

'Your blood is racing through your body like a gazelle fleeing from the hunter.'

'You…you startled me. I thought you were asleep!'

She winced a little as he released her, gritting a soft expletive under his breath. Moving with the swift stealth of a panther, throwing back the bedclothes, he reached out to relight the oil lamp on the table beside the bed, taunting her softly, 'If you thought I was asleep then what exactly are you doing here?'

Far from being asleep, he sounded dangerously alert, Petra recognised.

As she gave a small nervous shudder his expression changed abruptly. Frowningly he questioned her, 'What is it? What's wrong? Don't you feel well? The desert air can sometimes…'

'I'm fine,' Petra assured him quickly. 'It isn't…' Catching her bottom lip between her teeth, she struggled to drag her distracted…besotted gaze away from his naked torso. Like her, he obviously did not favour pyjamas. But unlike her, she suspected, from the brief glimpse she had just had of one lean muscular hip and the telltale dark shadowing of hair running down over his taut flat stomach, Blaize did not even adopt the modesty of wearing briefs to sleep in!

'Fine?' he repeated. 'Then what…?'

He looked fully awake now. And fully alert too, Petra recognised with a sinking, almost queasy sensation gripping her stomach. Thinking about delivering a short but noble speech of apology in the privacy of her own bed was one thing: actually doing it whilst she was poised semi-crouched on the edge of Blaize's bed, with her mind more on the fact that he was undoubtedly naked beneath the silky throw than on what she was supposed to be doing, was very much another! And if she wasn't careful…if she wasn't very, very careful indeed…she might just be in grave danger of totally ignoring what she had come here to do…

The scratches on Blaize's upper arm caught her attention. They had stopped bleeding but they still looked raw, and even slightly inflamed.

As she dragged her gaze away it met Blaize's, and was held there trapped…hypnotised…

'For your information, they were *not* caused by Shara…the dancer,' he told her quietly. 'The falconer had a new young bird he was training and it became over-excited. I offered to help him.' He gave a small shrug. 'As I told him, once she matures she will make an enviably loyal bird. She resented being handled by someone who was not her master and she let me know it.'

'A falcon scratched you?' Petra breathed, her face flooding with guilty colour. Now she owed him not one but two apologies.

Helplessly she looked back to his arm, and then, unable to stop herself, she leaned forward and gently caressed the broken skin with her lips, tenderly kissing the line of each scratch.

As she kissed the last one she felt Blaize's body quiver. Sombrely she turned her head and looked into his eyes.

'I came to apologise,' she told him quietly. 'I should not have…have done what I did.'

There was a small tense pause through which she could feel her own emotions pulsing, as though they possessed a life force of their own, whilst she waited for him to speak, and once again she found that she was having to wet her dry lips.

His thickly groaned, 'Don't do that, Petra!' followed by an even thicker, 'Why…why did you have to come in here?' drove the colour from her face, redefining the delicacy of her bone structure and highlighting her fragility. She started to move away, her eyes widening as Blaize followed her, grasping hold of her wrists and holding them against his bare chest as he looked deep into her eyes, before his gaze dropped, heavy-lidded with sensuality, to her mouth.

In the thick, taut silence that enveloped them while Blaize lit the lamp next to the bed Petra made the interesting scientific discovery that it was possible to find that one could not breathe even with open airways, parted lips, and an ample supply of oxygen!

'You know that you shouldn't really be here, don't you, my little virgin?'

His little virgin? Petra's heart jumped like a hooked fish throwing itself against her ribcage.

'I…'

I can go, Petra had been about to say. But speech had suddenly become impossible because Blaize was kissing her…kissing her with a mind-drugging, slow, sweet simplicity that was nothing more than the merest touch of his lips against hers, over and over again, and then again, until all she wanted to do was live off their touch, to feel it for ever.

Somehow she was now kneeling upright on the bed, and

so too was Blaize, so that they were body to body. His naked body next to her very scantily clad one!

Petra could feel the heavy, fierce thud of his heart beneath her hands as he held them against his chest.

He was kissing the tip of her nose, her closed eyelids, with tiny butterfly kisses that brushed the taut planes of her cheekbones whilst the hands pinning her own set them free, lifted to cup her face, to push the hair back from it so that his lips and then his tongue could investigate the delicate and oh, so sensually sensitive whorls of her ears.

Petra heard herself whimpering, an unfamiliar distant sound that was a needy plea for even more of the pleasure he was inflicting on her. Blindly she turned her head, seeking the warmth of his mouth.

His hands shaped her throat, holding it, his thumb measuring the frantic leaping pulse at its base. Her small curled fists still lay against his chest, the rasp of his body hair against her skin disturbingly sexual.

His hands were on her shoulders, beneath her wrap, stroking her skin, sliding the fabric away.

In the soft light of the lamp he had lit Petra could see their reflection in a mirror. Her skin looked milky pale against the warm tan of his, her breasts surely swollen, its taut peak surely a deeper, hotter colour as it pressed against him, flushed and pulsing with the desire that ached right through her.

If he were to touch her there now, cup her breast, roll his fingertip around her nipple... Her whole body stiffened in response to her own thoughts and it was as though somehow he had read her mind and felt her desires. His hand cupped her breast and his mouth returned to hers, his lips brushing over it with tantalising and then tormenting delicacy, making her lips part with hungry longing and her body press into his.

Wantonly she ran her tongue-tip over his lips, until he captured it and drew it between his teeth, caressing it with his own before his tongue slid deeper and deeper into the moist sweetness of her mouth.

As she moaned her pleasure deep in her throat, Petra felt him jerk away from her.

'Petra, no!' he told her thickly. 'This isn't—'

Not wanting to hear what he was obviously going to say, Petra put her fingertips to his lips, silencing him, kissing his face wildly, with fierce, impassioned little kisses as she breathed in his ear, 'Yes… Yes, it is!'

Removing her fingers, she pressed her mouth to his, her body to his, rubbing herself sensuously against him. Virgin she might be, but that did not mean she didn't understand what passion was…what wanting him was!

As she slid her hands over his body, helpless to stop herself, she felt him tense and then shudder. His skin felt like hot oiled satin, and Petra knew she could never, ever get enough of the feel of it beneath her hands. She kissed his throat, lingering over the place where his Adam's apple pressed hard against his skin, stroking it with her tongue, nibbling at his skin, taunting him with her desire and daring him to refuse to share it.

When he didn't move she curled her fingers in the soft thick hair on his body, tugging wantonly on it and flicking her tongue against the tiny peak of his flat male nipple.

'Petra, you are a virgin,' she heard him protesting rawly. 'I can't…'

As she abandoned her torment of his throat, and her lips moved down along the line of hair toward his stomach, she could almost hear him grinding his teeth. Her tongue rimmed his flat belly button, her love for him filling her with a sensual bravado that normally would have shocked her. She had never dreamed that the first time she made love she would be the one taking the initiative, making moves so bold and provocative that they shocked her almost as much as they excited her.

'I don't want—' she heard Blaize groan thickly.

But her fingertips were already exploring the taut strength of his arousal, lending her the confidence to whisper daringly, 'Oh, yes, you do,' before returning to her task of laving the maleness of his flat belly with her inquisitive tongue.

There was a muscle pulsing there that fascinated and compelled her. Wickedly she traced it with lingering appreciation, so raptly lost in the pleasure of what she was doing that it caught her completely off guard when Blaize suddenly took hold of her, depositing her on the bed and holding her there whilst he looked down at her, his gaze skimming her face and then her body, her breasts, her narrow waist. She saw him frown and looked down at her own flesh, realising that he was staring at the tiny diamond glinting in her belly.

'Who gave you that?' she heard him demanding fiercely.

For a few seconds Petra was bemused, and her fingertip touched the diamond in confusion.

'Who was he, Petra?' she heard Blaize reiterating savagely—so savagely, in fact, that she was unable to prevent the entirely female thrill of excited pleasure rippling through her. He was jealous! She could tell. For a heartbeat she fantasised about pretending that he had a rival, that another man had looked at her body and laid claim to it, put his badge of possession on it. But her natural honesty reasserted itself.

'I bought it myself—for myself!' she told him truthfully. 'I heard a couple of girls discussing me at a party, saying that I was the type of person who was too pure and naïve to wear anything like this, and so...' She gave a small dismissive shrug.

'This is a gift that only a man would give a woman,' Blaize was insisting, his eyes smokily charcoal, hot with male possession and desire.

'Not these days,' Petra contradicted him wryly.

'Then where else have you adorned yourself?' Blaize was demanding softly, and his hand moved lower down her body, his head bent over her.

Now it was his turn to torment her, to kiss her with surely far more expertise and deliberate enticement and sensuality than she had done him as he traced a line of kisses from her breastbone right down to her quivering belly.

As she had done to him he rimmed her navel with tiny kisses, and then the tip of his tongue, but then, before Petra could stop him, he tugged delicately on the diamond whilst his hand covered her sex, his thumb slowly probing an entrance between its tightly furled outer covering in a way that made her heart turn over inside her chest whilst the whole of her body turned molten and fluid with arousal.

'Nowhere else,' she heard herself whisper, but even as she said them she knew that the words were not needed, that Blaize had discovered for himself that her body possessed no other form of adornment!

Withdrawing slightly, he looked down at her whilst she quivered from head to foot—but not with apprehension or regret.

'I want you,' she told him huskily. 'I want you now, Blaize.'

But as she reached for him he shook his head.

'Wait!' he told her, reaching out to open a small cupboard beside the bed.

'I just hope that whoever planned this as a lovers' retreat did some proper forward planning,' Petra heard him mutter.

Bewildered, she waited, trying to peer past his shoulder, and then when she did see what he had been searching for her face coloured self-consciously.

Until now all 'safe sex' had meant to her was an expression that applied to other people!

But of course Blaize was more experienced, far more worldly than she was herself, and shakily she admitted that she was thankful that he was being so conscientious!

She even felt a tiny little thrill of excitement, knowing what he was doing, what it was leading up to! And when he was ready and he turned back to her, wrapping her in his arms and kissing her slowly and thoroughly before caressing her body, she shivered in passionate urgency.

She had thought that she knew what wanting him, aching for him felt like! But she had been wrong!

Enshrined in the street lore of her girlhood, the received wisdom of a hundred magazine articles and books, she had carried a certain protective wisdom that 'first times were not good times'—but she had been wrong about that too!

She hadn't known just how proactive her own role would be, how proactive she would want it to be as she reached and touched, stretched and invited, as she shuddered in the exquisite indescribable sensation of having him slowly enter her, slowly fill her...

But she knew now.

She hadn't known either how easily she would find the words she could hear echoing the pace of his deepening thrusts, which told him all that she was feeling and wanting.

But she knew that now too.

Every breath he took as he filled and completed her— against her skin, in her ear, in the thud of his heartbeat against her own, deep inside her body, where it radiated out in golden waves—was the breath of life itself.

And then, just as she thought she had accustomed herself

totally to the feel of him, he changed the pace, increasing its intensity, deepening it, letting her feel the strength of its power, letting her see that her body was ready for such intimacy.

And it was!

Mindlessly Petra clung to him, lifting herself against him so that he could go deeper, fuller, stronger, so that the intimacy they were sharing was so intense, so sweetly, savagely unbearable that it had to shatter, hurling them both through paroxysm after paroxysm of pleasure and into the beautiful golden peace that lay beyond it.

'Mmm.' Sleepily, Petra drew a small heart on the smooth skin of Blaize's bare shoulder with her fingertip. He was asleep and she could see the dark fans his eyelashes made against the warmth of his tanned skin in the soft light of the lamp. She had been asleep herself until a couple of minutes ago, but it seemed that her body didn't want to waste a moment of the time it could have with Blaize in sleep when she could be awake, watching him, touching him…loving him.

There—she had acknowledged her love! Admitted it! Accepted it?

She closed her eyes, testing the words inside her head. I love him. I love Blaize.

Yes, it was true. She could tell that from the way her whole being responded to the inner vibration of the words. She loved him! She loved Blaize.

She moved closer to him, bending her head to replace her fingertip with her lips, slowly retracing her heart with tiny whisper-light kisses.

His skin felt so warm, his body so excitingly different from her own and yet now so wonderfully, preciously familiar.

From now until the very end of her life she would re-member tonight. Until the day she died she would be able to close her eyes and recreate his image inside her head. Her hands would never forget what it had felt like to touch him; her lips would never forget the taste of his, the heat of his mouth, the way he had kissed her.

Her eyes soft and dark with her own emotions, Petra traced the shape of his arm and then the length of his back, the curve of his buttock.

'Two can play at this game.'

Petra gasped as Blaize's hand suddenly slid over her, down to her waist and then up again to cup her breast, whilst his voice echoed in her ear.

'You wouldn't be trying to take advantage of a sleeping man, would you?' he teased her.

'I just wanted to see if you felt as good as I remembered,' Petra told him honestly.

She felt him move, tensing a little, as though her words had somehow touched a raw nerve, or were something he didn't really want to hear. But she decided that she must be wrong when he demanded, 'And do I?'

As he spoke his thumb was deliberately teasing the un-expectedly taut and excited peak of her breast.

The shock of discovering how easily and quickly he could make her feel so hungry for him distracted her. Her hands were already curling, weaving rhythmically against his skin as her body started to pulse and ache.

Eagerly she kissed his throat and then his mouth, making a soft, taut sound of need deep in her throat as she pulled his head down towards her breast.

The sensation of his lips covering her nipple, caressing it, drawing it deeper into his mouth, made her dig her fin-gers into the hard muscles of his back. Already she was imagining the feel of him inside her, aching for it and for him, so much that she reached out and ran her fingertips down his body, touching him with a knowing intimacy that would have shocked her twenty-four hours ago.

Against her breast he made a sound she couldn't decipher, smothered by the urgency of her compelling need as she arched against him and gloried in the swelling hardness of the male flesh beneath her touch.

Blaize had released her breast and rolled onto his back. She felt his hands on her waist. To lift her away? Swiftly she bent her head towards his body, her lips touching the hard shaft of flesh that compelled her, that she knew would complete her!

'Petra…Petra…'

Her name was a raw, tormented sound of broken male control that filled her with sweetly savage pleasure.

His hands were still on her waist, but this time as he lifted her it was not away from him but towards him.

As he positioned her Petra shuddered, her eyes huge and dark with the realisation of how quickly and wantonly her body had adjusted to its newly dominant role.

Slickly they moved together, deeper, stronger, faster, whilst she stared into the mask of agonised pleasure that was Blaize's face, his need openly revealed to her as he cried out and his body jerked in fierce spasms just as the pleasure exploded inside her.

She was trembling so much that she couldn't move, couldn't do anything other than lie against him whilst he wrapped his arms around her and rocked her.

'That shouldn't have happened,' she heard him telling her in a voice that was raw with emotions she didn't have the energy to analyse as a fog of exhaustion enveloped her.

'That should *not* have happened,' he repeated.

'Yuck, camel's milk! How totally disgusting!'

Petra forced herself to try and smile as the girl next to

her, sharing the communal breakfast they had been served at the tourist village, turned towards her, waiting for her to respond to her friendly comment.

Ordinarily Petra knew that she would have enjoyed joining in the good-natured atmosphere of the alfresco breakfast they had been served. But when she had woken up this morning she had woken up alone and in her own bed!

Blaize must have carried her there whilst she was asleep. Why hadn't he wanted her to stay with him? Why hadn't he wanted to keep her with him?

Now last night's euphoria had disappeared, leaving her feeling frighteningly hollow and cold inside.

What she needed right now more than anything else was Blaize's presence, Blaize's reassurance—and most of all Blaize's love!

CHAPTER EIGHT

'THANKS for the lift...'

Petra watched as the young tour guide reiterated his grateful thanks to Blaize, before jumping down out of the Land Rover.

They had all been on the point of departing from the oasis when the tour guide's Jeep had refused to start.

Places had been found for his passengers in other vehicles, but unfortunately there had not been enough room for him, so Blaize had offered to give him a lift back to the complex.

Of course his presence had made it impossible for Petra and Blaize to discuss anything personal, but Petra suspected that she minded this far more than Blaize did.

The truth was that he was probably relieved she couldn't say anything about last night, Petra acknowledged unhappily.

After all, if he had felt anything for her—even a mere small percentage of the love she knew she had for him—then he would have told her so last night, instead of returning her to her own bed and then treating her this morning as though...as though she meant nothing to him!

She might mean nothing to him, but he meant everything to her!

Still, at least one good thing had come out of last night, she tried to tell herself with a brave attempt at cynical courage.

Rashid certainly wasn't going to want to marry her now. Not once he knew she had spent the night with another man! Given herself to another man! A man, moreover, who didn't love or want her!

Determinedly Petra tried not to give in to her own despair.

That wasn't true, she argued mentally with herself. Blaize had wanted her!

Her or just a woman…any woman?

Her pain was so intense that she didn't dare to even look at Blaize, just in case he might read her feelings in her eyes and feel even more contempt for her than he no doubt already did. All she meant to him was a meal ticket and a few hours of casual and no doubt quickly forgettable sex! She had known what he was all along, she reminded herself, so why had she been so stupid? So reckless with herself and her love? What had she been thinking? That with her he would be different? That her love would make it different? Why, why, why had she closed her eyes so deliberately to reality? Why had she ignored everything she knew about him and the way he lived his life?

Because her love for him had given her no choice, Petra recognised bleakly. Because, against her love, common sense and logic had no real weapons at all!

Acidly painful tears burned the back of Petra's throat. They were outside her hotel now, and without giving Blaize the opportunity to say anything she opened the door of the Land Rover and got out.

As she walked away she thought she heard Blaize calling her name, but she refused to stop.

It might be too late to stop herself from loving Blaize, but it was not too late for her to salvage her pride and her self-respect!

If she had meant anything to him…anything at all…he would have told her so last night.

*   *   *

An hour later, having exhausted every rational and several very irrational combinations of reasons and excuses for Blaize's behaviour, and still had to return to the unwanted, unbearable truth that he had simply been using her and, having done so now, no longer wanted her, Petra heard someone knocking on the door to her suite.

Immediately, despite everything she had just told herself, her heart leapt, whilst relief and joy poured through her. It was Blaize! It had to be! She had got it all wrong! There was a rational explanation for the distance he had put between them, and he had now come to explain everything to her—to apologise for hurting her and to tell her how much he wanted her, how much he loved her.

Her whole face illuminated with happiness and love, Petra ran to open the door.

Only it wasn't Blaize who was standing outside; it was her cousin Saud. In the shock of her disappointment Petra could only stand and stare at him uncomprehendingly.

'Are you packed yet?' she heard him asking her.

'Packed?'

'I told my mother she should have rung ahead to check that you were ready!'

Ready! Guiltily Petra realised that today was the day she was due to move in to the family villa. She had been so wrapped up in her love for Blaize and what had happened between them that she had totally overlooked the plans that had been made.

'I…I'm running a bit late, Saud,' she told him. After all, it was technically the truth. 'I'm sorry…'

'That's okay,' Saud assured her easily. 'I'm not in any rush. Did you enjoy your trip into the dessert with Rashid? I saw him driving you there,' he added casually.

Petra stared at him, her body completely immobile, like

that of someone caught up in the dark power of a sorcerer's spell.

'Rashid?' she questioned. Her lips were having trouble framing his name, and her heart had started to beat with heavy-doom laden thuds that rocked her whole body. 'You saw me with Rashid?'

'Yes, in one of the safari company's Land Rovers,' Saud confirmed.

'But I wasn't with—' Petra began to protest, and then stopped as Saud continued with a wide grin.

'My mother's already planning the wedding. She thinks...'

'Rashid,' Petra mouthed, forcing her lips to accommodate themselves to his name, whilst her body shook with the enormity of what Saud had said. 'But...'

But what? she asked herself numbly. But she had not been with Rashid. She had been with Blaize! Blaize who was not Rashid...who could not be Rashid...

'I suppose Rashid is working upstairs in the Presidential Suite now, is he?' Saud was chattering on happily. 'Has he taken you to see his new villa yet? The one he has just had built out by the private oasis he bought?' Saud was asking her excitedly. 'Did he show you his horses? And his falcons? I'd love a falcon of my own, but Dad says it's out of the question—especially if I'm to go to university in America.'

'Saud, I'm not...I'm not packed yet. Could you come back a little later, say in an hour?' she asked him jerkily, interrupting his enthusiastic and excited conversation.

'Sure!'

Petra stared blankly at the door Saud had closed behind him.

Saud had said that he had seen her with Rashid. But the

man she had been with was Blaize. Which meant either that Saud had been mistaken or...

There was a vile sickening sensation clawing coldly at the pit of her stomach, a suspicion inside her head that wouldn't go away.

The Presidential Suite. That was on the top floor. White-faced, but determined, Petra opened the door of her suite and headed for the lift.

What she was thinking couldn't be true, it just couldn't! Saud had to be mistaken, but she had to find out, she had to know...to be sure!

Only one lift went all the way to the Presidential Suite, and when she got out of it Petra was trembling violently—although whether from shock, fear or fury, she didn't really know.

Blaize could not be Rashid. It was totally implausible that he might be, totally impossible! But somehow the re-assurances she was trying to give herself had a disconcert-ingly hollow and empty sound to them.

In the private hallway to the suite, a thick, lushly rich carpet muffled her footsteps—but not her racing heartbeat. Nervously Petra stared at the closed door in front of her.

What was she doing here? Blaize was a beach bum, a chancer, an adventurer who lived on his wits and other people's money, a man with no moral beliefs, who made his own rules—and then broke them. Rashid, in contrast, from what she had heard about him, was a seriously suc-cessful businessman, a man ruthlessly focused on his own goals, a man prepared to marry a woman he did not know for his own advancement and benefit.

They could not be one and the same person. It was un-thinkable that they might be. Unthinkable, unsustainable, unendurable! Of course it was! Saud had simply made a mistake.

Feeling slightly calmer, Petra pressed the doorbell and waited.

The door swung inwards, and a male voice demanded curtly, 'Yes?'

The voice was the same, but the businesslike crispness certainly wasn't!

Her throat muscles virtually paralysed with shock and disbelief, Petra stared up into Blaize's face. Only he wasn't Blaize. He was... He was...

Ignoring the bare arm that Blaize had placed across the half-open doorway, Petra pushed her way past him and into the suite.

She had obviously disturbed Blaize, or rather Rashid, as she now knew him to be in mid-shower, to judge from the rivulets of moisture still running over his skin down to the towel he had draped round his hips.

'How could you?' she demanded chokily. 'How dare you? Why did you do it? Why...? Let go of me,' she spat as he suddenly took hold of her arm, her face white with shock and fury. 'Let go of me,' she repeated, as Blaize— Rashid, she corrected herself bitterly—virtually dragged her into the elegant sitting room.

If she had either shocked or shamed him, he certainly wasn't showing it.

'Not until you've calmed down and you're ready to listen to reason,' Rashid told her calmly. 'Come and sit down and I'll get you a cool drink. You look as though you need one.'

A cool drink! Petra tried to pull free of him and found that she could not.

'What I need,' she told him through gritted teeth, 'is an explanation of...of what is going on...of why you pretended to be someone you quite obviously are not...'

'I was going to tell you,' Rashid interrupted her curtly. 'But—'

'Liar!' Petra cut across him. 'You're lying to me. Just like you've lied to me all along! Let go of me,' she demanded fiercely. 'I can't bear having you touch me. I—'

'That wasn't what you said last night,' Rashid reminded her grimly.

Petra shuddered, unable to stop herself from reacting—not just to his words, but also to her own feelings, her memories…

'In fact, last night, as I recall, you seemed to find my touch a good deal more than merely bearable! Remember?'

When Petra refused to answer Rashid goaded her.

'Shall I help you to do so?'

As Petra gave a sharp gasp of shock he drew her closer to him. Petra tensed as she felt the dampness of his skin through her thin top. Her mind knew how gravely, how devastatingly, how unforgivably he had behaved towards her, but her body seemed only to know that he was its lover, its love.

'If I were to kiss you now,' he began softly, the words whispering tormentingly against her tightly closed lips, 'then…'

He stopped speaking and lifted his head as the suite door suddenly opened and a tall grey-bearded man strode in, his bearing immediately marking him out as a person of eminence and rank.

'Rashid, our new American project—how long do you think—' he began, and then stopped as he took in the scene in front of him, its apparent intimacy.

Eyes as sharp and dark as a falcon's made Petra feel as though she was as pinioned beneath their gaze as she was by Rashid's grip.

'Highness, please allow me to present to you Miss Petra Cabbot.'

Highness!

Petra gulped, sensing the cool air of regal disapproval emanating from the newcomer as he looked from Rashid to Petra and then back to Rashid again before saying quietly, 'I see!'

He left a brief but telling pause before asking Petra politely, 'Your godfather is well, I trust, Miss Cabbot? He and I were at Eton together.'

'He's—he's in the Far East,' Petra managed to croak, wondering if she dared add that he was there with her passport—which right now she needed very much.

'Indeed.' The princely head was inclined towards her. 'He is a very shrewd statesman, as was your father. Statesmen of world-class stature with far-seeing eyes are very much needed in these turbulent times.'

Her face burning, Petra moved out of earshot of the two men whilst the Prince spoke with Rashid.

Despite the Prince's politeness, Petra was uncomfortably aware of his evident, if unexpressed disapproval of her presence unchaperoned in Rashid's suite.

The moment the Prince had left, Petra made to leave herself. But immediately Rashid shook his head, closing the door firmly and standing in front of it as he said grimly, 'You do realise what this means, don't you? What will have to happen now that the Prince has seen you here alone with me?'

'You were the one who introduced me to him,' Petra reminded him defensively, ignoring his question.

'Because I had no other option,' Rashid told her savagely. 'If I had chosen not to introduce you it would have been a tacit admission that it was because honourably I could not do so...because you were my whore! There is

nothing else for it now. You will have to marry me!
Nothing less can save your reputation or that of your family!'

Petra stared at him in shocked disbelief.

'What?' she croaked. 'We can't!'

'We can and we are,' Rashid assured her grimly. 'In fact,
we don't have any other option—thanks to you!'

'Thanks to me?' Petra glared at him. 'Thanks to me?
What does that mean? I wasn't the one...'

'It means that since His Highness found you here in my
apartment unchaperoned, I now have no other option than
to marry you. It was obvious what he thought.'

'What...? That's...that's ridiculous,' Petra protested.
'Why didn't you just tell him the truth?'

'Which truth?' Rashid demanded scornfully. 'The truth
that says last night you gave yourself to me? Last night...'

'Stop it...stop it.' Petra demanded in anguish, before accusing him recklessly, 'You've done all this deliberately,
haven't you? Just so that you can get your own way and
force me to marry you—for the financial benefit you'll get
out of it! Just as a matter of interest, what is marriage to
me worth to you, Rashid?' Her temper was burning white-
hot. 'A good deal more than the traditional camels, I am
sure! One hotel...two...an office block and perhaps a
dozen or more villas thrown in? And why stop there? I
know that the Royal Family's hotel interests extend all over
the world, and—'

'You're overreacting.' Rashid cut across her increasingly
emotional words curtly. 'If you would just allow me to
explain—'

'Explain what?' Petra demanded bitterly. 'Explain that
you deliberately lied to me and...and plotted and planned
to...to use me for...for your own ends?'

'Me—use *you*. I wasn't the one who came into your

room,' Rashid reminded her icily. 'Into your bed! If anything, if anyone is to blame for the situation we now find ourselves in, Petra, it is you and your wretched virginal curiosity! And, contrary to what your juvenile imagination has decided, it is for that reason that I have no option other than to do the honourable thing and marry you.'

'Because I was a virgin! That's crazy!'

'No. You are crazy if you honestly believe there can be any other outcome to what happened. We have to marry now. Apart from any other consideration there is the fact that you could have a child.'

Petra stared at him.

'But...but that isn't possible,' she started to stammer. 'You...you...took precautions...'

She tensed as she heard him draw an exaggeratedly deep breath.

'Indeed I did—the first time!' he told her derisively. 'The second time I did not, and the second time I...'

'You planned all this, didn't you?' Petra repeated furiously, panicked by both the situation and Rashid's grim anger. 'You deliberately lied to me and—'

'Do you really think I like or want this any more than you do? And as for planning it! You obviously haven't listened properly to me, Petra. As I've just told you, I wasn't the one who crawled into your bed! Nor was I the one who begged—'

With a small chagrined moan Petra forced back the shocked emotional tears that were already stinging her eyes.

'How many more times do I have to tell you that for me not to marry you now would not just relegate you to the status of a...a plaything, it would humiliate your grandfather and his whole family?' Rashid said bitingly. 'Quite apart from the fact that you were alone in here with me in an intimate situation—do you really think the fact that we spent the night together last night went unnoticed? Has it really not occurred to you yet that this morning you so obviously looked...'

'No! I won't listen to any more,' she protested.

Every word he said was like a knife in her heart. She could hardly take in what was happening. What he had said. She had enough to do trying to come to terms with the fact that the man she had thought of as Blaize was in actual fact someone quite different, without having to cope with this additional shock!

'None of this need have happened if you had just been honest with me that evening down on the beach,' she threw at him wildly. 'If you had told me then.'

'When you first approached me I had no idea who you were. I had just returned from a business trip to discover that the idiotic young man who looked after the windsurfers, who I had already had to warn on more than one occasion about his familiarity with the female guests, had been discovered by one of our guests in bed with his wife. Naturally I had had to sack him, and I had gone down to the beach simply to walk and think.'

'You were putting away the windsurfers,' Petra accused him bitterly.

Rashid gave a small shrug.

'An automatic habit. I worked on a Californian beach as a student, and just seeing them lying untidily there...'

'You could have told me who you were! Stopped me...' Petra persisted. 'You may think that you have been very clever, tricking me like this, but I won't marry you, Rashid.'

'You don't have any other choice,' he told her starkly. 'Neither of us do! Not now! I cannot—'

'You cannot what?' Petra demanded, refusing to allow him to finish speaking. 'You cannot afford to offend the

Royal Family? Well…well, tough! No way am I going to marry you just to…to save your precious reputation—'

She stopped in mid-sentence as Rashid cut across her, his voice sharply cynical. '*My* reputation? Haven't you listened to anything I have just said? It is your own you should be thinking about! Your own and that of your family. Because what I cannot do, Petra, unless I marry you, is protect you from the gossip that is now bound to occur. And not just about you! I have far too much respect for your grandfather to want to publicly humiliate him by having it known that I have not offered you marriage.'

'Fine! Your conscience is clear, Rashid! You have offered me marriage. And I am refusing to accept!'

'Despite the fact that you could be carrying my child?'

For a moment they looked at one another. Petra could feel herself weakening, remembering… But then she made herself face reality. He had lied to her, totally and without compunction, tricked and deceived her, and she could never overlook that, not if she wanted to retain her own self-respect, what little there was left of it!

Determinedly she told him, 'It could also be that I am not carrying your child! I won't marry you, Rashid,' she reinforced.

'Unfortunately, I am tied up with business meetings which cannot be cancelled or delayed until the day after tomorrow. But rest assured, Petra, on that day I shall be calling on your grandfather to formally request your hand in marriage.'

So intense was her sense of fury and frustration that Petra simply couldn't speak. Giving Rashid a savagely bitter look, she headed for the door.

To her relief he allowed her to pass through it without making any attempt to stop her or to say anything else.

Calling on her grandfather to request her hand in marriage. She had never heard of anything so archaic! Well, she would soon make it plain to him that his proposal was neither wanted nor acceptable!

CHAPTER NINE

'AUNT SORAYA,' Petra exclaimed warmly as she saw her aunt approaching her. 'I thought you were going out to spend the day with your friend.'

Her aunt had already told Petra with some excitement that she had been invited to visit an old schoolfriend whose daughter had just become betrothed to an extremely wealthy and highly placed prince.

To Petra's concern her aunt immediately looked not merely flustered but also acutely distressed, with large tears filling her soft brown eyes.

Taking hold of her hands in her own, Petra begged her, 'Aunt, what is it? What's wrong? Please tell me—has something happened to your friend or her daughter?'

Emotionally her aunt shook her head.

'Please,' Petra urged her. 'Tell me what's wrong?'

She had, she realised, become closer to her aunt than she had imagined she would, and the older woman's air of vulnerability made her feel very protective of her.

'Petra. I did not wish to tell you this,' her aunt was saying unhappily. 'The last thing I want to do is to hurt or anger you.'

Hurt or anger her?

Petra began to frown as a cold finger of icy intuition pressed warningly against her spine.

'I was to have seen my friend and her daughter today,' her aunt admitted, 'But she has telephoned to say that the visit must be cancelled. It is nothing personal against you, Petra. At least not intentionally! My friend understands that you did not mean to… Well, she knows you have had a European upbringing. It is just that she has her daughter to protect, and the family of her husband-to-be are…are very traditional in their outlook…'

She was beginning to stumble slightly over her explanation in very obvious embarrassment, but Petra had already guessed what was coming.

Even so it was still a shock to have her aunt confirm her fears.

'There has been gossip about you, Petra! I know, of course, that there will be a perfectly acceptable reason for…for…everything…but my friend has heard that you are known to have been alone with Rashid, and that you and he—'

She broke off, blinking away her tears and pressing her hand to her mouth as though she could hardly bring herself to say any more.

'I cannot believe that Rashid would knowingly behave in such a way, that he would expose you to…that he should not behave honourably and…'

'Offer to marry me?' Petra suggested grimly. 'Well, as a matter of fact, Aunt, that is exactly what he has done. Although I…'

'He has!' Suddenly her aunt's face was wreathed in a relieved smile. Reaching out, she hugged Petra warmly, patently oblivious to the cynicism Petra had been intending to convey in her voice. 'Oh, Petra I am so happy… So overjoyed for you…for you both. He will make you a wonderful husband. Your grandfather will be so very very pleased.'

'No, Aunt, you don't understand,' Petra tried to protest, suddenly beginning to panic as she realised the interpretation her aunt had put on her admission. It was one thing for her to tell her aunt for the sake of her own pride and her aunt's comfort that Rashid had offered to marry her, but she had never intended that her aunt should assume she was pleased or, more importantly, that she actually intended to accept.

However, having made her own interpretation of Petra's words her aunt proved stubbornly hard to change!

Rashid had proposed! Of course it was impossible that Petra might have refused, and every attempt Petra made to tell her that she had done just that was greeted with amused laugher and comments about Petra's 'teasing' until Petra herself fell silent in despairing exasperation.

'I should have trusted Rashid, of course,' her aunt was saying. 'Although it was very thoughtless of you both to put your reputation at so much risk, Petra. Your mother would have hated knowing that people were beginning to talk about you the way they were,' she reproved her gently.

Her mother! Petra's heart suddenly ached. Her mother would have hated knowing that her daughter's name was being bandied about in a scurrilous way, that was true, but she would not have condemned her for what had happened. Petra knew that as well.

'So, you and Rashid are betrothed,' her aunt was saying happily. 'We are going to be so busy, Petra. Oh, my, dear,' she said, giving Petra another hug. 'I had not meant to tell you this, but now that you have put my mind at ease with the news of your betrothal I feel that I can. Had Rashid not offered you marriage, it would have done our family a very great deal of harm, and lowered our standing in the community to such an extent that my own husband's business would have been badly affected—as would your cousin's chances of making a good marriage. And as for your grandfather... I do not exaggerate, Petra, when I tell you that I think the shame might have killed him.'

Killed him!

Petra stood frozen within her aunt's warm embrace, feeling as though she had suddenly walked into a trap which had sprung so tightly around her that she would never be able to escape. And it made no difference at all that she had unwittingly and foolishly been the one to spring that trap herself!

There was no way out for her now. For the sake of her family she had no alternative other than to marry Rashid!

'Oh, Petra! You look so beautiful,' her aunt whispered emotionally. 'A perfect bride.'

They were standing together in Petra's bedroom at the family villa, waiting for Petra's grandfather to escort her to the civil marriage ceremony that would make her Rashid's wife.

After the civil ceremony there was to be a lavish banquet held in their honour in the specially decorated banqueting suite of the hotel.

Petra's aunt had spent virtually the whole of the last three days there overseeing everything, along with some of Rashid's female relatives, but despite her exhortations Petra had not been able to bring herself to go and view the scene of her own legal entrapment.

There was no point, she knew, in trying to tell her aunt that she did not want to marry Rashid. The older woman had a ridiculously high opinion of him and would, Petra knew, simply not be able to accept that Petra herself hated and despised him.

Rashid knew it, though—she had made sure of that the day he had come to formally ask her grandfather for her hand in marriage.

Unable to refuse him outright as she had wished, for the sake of her aunt and her family, she had had to content herself with a bitterly contemptuous and hostile glare at him when her grandfather had summoned her to receive his proposal.

'I am pleased to see that you have had the good sense to realise there is no alternative to this—for either of us,' he had managed to tell her grimly, gritting the words to her so quietly that no one else could hear them.

And, as though that hadn't been bad enough, she had then had to endure the miserable, humiliating parody of being forced to pretend that she wanted to accept his proposal!

However, she had managed to avert her face when he had leaned towards her to kiss her, so that his mouth had merely grazed her cheek instead of touching her lips.

Beneath his breath he had taunted her, 'How very modest! A traditional shrinking bride! However, I already know just how passionate you can be beneath that assumed cold exterior!'

And now there was no escape for her.

Her attendants—a swarm of pretty chattering girls from her aunt's extended family and Rashid's—had already left for the hotel in their stunning butterfly-hued outfits, and soon Petra herself would be leaving with her grandfather. She tensed as her bedroom door opened and her grandfather came in.

Giving her veil a final twitch, her aunt left them on their own.

As he came towards her Petra could see that her grandfather's eyes were shining with emotion. 'You are so like your mother,' he whispered. 'Every day I see more and more of her in you. I have something I would like you to wear today,' he told her abruptly, producing a leather jewellery box and removing from it a diamond necklace of such delicate workmanship that Petra couldn't help giving a small murmur of appreciation.

'This is for you,' she heard her grandfather telling her. 'It would mean a great deal to me if you would wear it today, Petra.'

Now Petra could understand her aunt's insistence on choosing a fabric for her wedding gown which was sewn with tiny crystals. Originally, when the silk merchant had come to the house with a selection of fabrics, Petra had wondered bitterly just what kind of fabric would best suit a sacrificial offering. It had been her aunt who had fallen on the heavy matt cream fabric with its scattering of tiny beads with an exclamation of triumph.

Petra could feel her grandfather's hands shaking as he fastened the necklace for her. It fitted her so perfectly that it might have been made for her.

'It was your mother's,' he said. 'It was my last gift to her. She left it behind. She would have been so proud of you today, Petra. Both your parents would, and with good reason.'

Proud of her? For allowing herself to be tricked into a soulless, loveless marriage?

Panic suddenly filled her. She couldn't marry Rashid. She wouldn't! She turned to her grandfather, but before she could speak her aunt came back into the room.

'It is time for you to leave,' she told them both.

As her grandfather walked towards the stairs Petra made to follow him, but her aunt suddenly stopped her. 'You are not wearing Rashid's gift,' she chided her.

Petra stared at her.

'The perfume he sent you, which he had specially blended for you,' her aunt reminded her, clicking her tongue as she hurried over to the table and picked up the heavy crystal bottle.

'No…I don't want to wear it…' Petra started to say, but her aunt wasn't listening to her.

Petra froze as the warm, sensual scent surrounded her in a fragrant cloud.

'It is perfect for you,' her aunt was saying. 'It has the youthfulness of innocence and the maturity of womanliness. Rashid has chosen well. And your mother's necklace is perfect on you, Petra. Your grandfather has never stopped missing her or loving her, you know.'

As her throat threatened to close up with tears, Petra demanded huskily, 'If he loved her so much then why didn't he at least come to the funeral? Even if he could not have been there he could have sent a message… something…anything…'

All the pain she had felt on that dreadful day, when she had stood at her parents' graveside surrounded by their friends and her father's family and yet feeling dreadfully alone, was in her voice.

She heard her aunt sigh.

'Petra, he would have been there. But there was his heart attack—and then when your godfather wrote that he did not think it a good idea that you should come here to us, that you had your own life and friends, he was too proud to…to risk a second rejection.'

Petra stared at her. She had known that her grandfather had made a very belated and seemingly—to her—very reluctant offer to give her a home, following her parents' death, but she had had no idea that he had been prevented from attending their funeral by a heart attack.

'A heart attack?' she faltered. 'I…'

'It was his second,' her aunt informed her, and then suddenly looked acutely uncomfortable, as though she had said something she should not have said.

'His second?' Petra had known nothing of this. 'Then…when…when did he have his first?' she demanded with a small frown.

Her aunt was becoming increasingly agitated.

'Petra, I should not have spoken of this. Your grandfather never wanted... He swore us all to secrecy when it happened because he didn't want your mother to feel...'

'My mother?'

She gave her aunt a determined look.

'I am not leaving this room until you tell me everything,' she informed her sturdily.

'Petra, you will be late. The car is waiting, and your grandfather...'

'Not one single step,' Petra warned her.

'Oh, dear. I should never... Very well, then. I suppose it can do no harm for you to know now...after all, it was your mother your grandfather wanted to protect. He loved her so much, you see, Petra... He loved his sons, of course, but he had that love for her that a father will often have for his girl-child. According to my husband he spoiled her outrageously, but then I suppose that is an older brother speaking. When she left like that, your grandfather was beside himself...with anger...and with despair. He had planned so much for her...

'Your uncle—my husband—found him slumped across his desk, holding your mother's photograph. The doctor did not think he would survive. He was ill for a very, very long time. Oh...I should not have told you—not today,' her aunt said remorsefully as she saw how pale Petra had gone.

'All those wasted years,' Petra whispered. 'When they could have been together—when we could all have been together as a family!'

'He missed her dreadfully.'

'But my father wrote, sent photographs...'

Her aunt sighed.

'You have to understand, Petra. Your grandfather is a very proud man. He couldn't bear to accept an olive branch extended by your father. He wanted…needed to know that your mother still wanted him in her life, that she still loved him.'

'She believed that he would never forgive her,' Petra told her chokily, shaking her head.

'When the news came that your parents were dead, your grandfather…' Her aunt paused and shook her head. 'It was a terrible, terrible time for him, Petra. He couldn't believe it. Wouldn't accept that she was gone, that he had lost her. When he had his second heart attack we honestly believed that it was in part because he simply no longer wanted to live. But mercifully he recovered. It was his greatest wish then that you might come to us, but your godfather—wisely, perhaps, in the circumstances, thought it best for you that you remained in an environment that was familiar to you. But your grandfather never gave up hoping, and when he knew that your uncle was to meet your godfather he begged him to try to persuade you to come here. I can't tell you how happy you are making him today, Petra. I wish you every happiness, my dearest girl, for you most certainly deserve it.'

As her aunt leaned forward to embrace her Petra felt her eyes burn with emotional tears.

In a daze she made her way out to the waiting car and her grandfather. Suddenly she was seeing him with new eyes. Loving, compassionate eyes. As she sat beside him she reached out and touched his hand. Immediately he clasped hers.

'You may kiss the bride!'

Petra felt her whole body clench against the pain of what was happening. Unable to move, she felt the coldness thrown by Rashid's shadow as he bent towards her.

She waited until the last possible second to turn her head

away, so that his dutiful kiss would only brush her cheek and not her lips. But to her shock, as though he had known what she would do, as she moved so did he, lifting his hand so that to their audience it looked at though he were cupping the side of her face in the most tender gesture of a lover, unable to stop himself from imbuing even this, a formal public rite, with the possessive adoration of a man deeply in love.

Only she knew that what he was actually doing was preventing her from turning away from him, that he was reinforcing to her his right, his legally given right as her husband, to demand her physical acceptance of him.

His mouth touched hers, and she trembled visibly with the force of her anger. She had believed in him, trusted him, loved him, but all the time he had been deceiving her, lying to her. How could she ever trust her own judgement again?

She would have to be constantly on her guard against it! And against him?

He moved, the smallest gesture that brought his nose against hers in the merest little touch, as though he wanted to offer her comfort and reassurance. Another lie…another deceit…and yet for an instant, caught up in the intensity of the moment, she had almost swayed yearningly towards him, wanting it to be real!

Suddenly Petra felt desperately afraid. She had thought in her ignorance that it would be enough simply for her to know what Rashid was to stop herself from continuing to love him, but now, shockingly, she wasn't so sure!

She hated him for what he had done; she knew that! So why did he still have the power to move her physically, to make her want him?

What was she thinking? Was she going crazy? She did

not want him. Not one tiny little bit! Fiercely she pushed against him. To her relief he released her immediately.

The ceremony was over. They were man and wife!

'I never knew that Rashid's middle name was Blaize.' That was her cousin Saud, flushed and excited, openly proud of his new relationship with his hero.

'Petra, my dear, your father would have been so proud had he been here today.'

Numbly Petra smiled automatically at the American Ambassador.

'Petra, you look so breathtakingly beautiful,' his wife, an elegant Texan with a slow drawl said with a warm smile. 'Doesn't she Rashid?' she demanded, causing Petra to stiffen, the tiny hairs on the back of her neck lifting as Rashid turned to look at her.

'She is my heart's desire,' Rashid responded quietly, without taking his gaze off her.

'Petra, take him away and hide him before I turn green, you lucky girl,' the Ambassador's wife teased.

'I am the one who is lucky,' Rashid corrected her.

'He certainly is,' Petra chimed in brittly. 'Today he isn't just gaining a wife, are you, Rashid? He's gaining the opportunity to design a new multi-million-pound-complex, and—'

'I'm certainly going to need some good commissions if I'm to keep you in the style your grandfather is accustoming you to.' Rashid cut across her outburst in a light drawl that masked the icy, glittering look of warning only she could see. 'At least if that necklace you're wearing is anything to go by.'

'Yes, it's gorgeous,' another of the guests enthused.

Petra tensed as she felt Rashid's hand beneath her elbow.

'I don't know why you're so determined to play the adoring husband,' she told him bitterly.

'No, I don't suppose you do,' he agreed.

'Why didn't you tell me that your second name was Blaize?'

He gave a small dismissive shrug.

'Does is it matter? Rashid or Blaize—I am still the same man, Petra. The man who—'

'The man who lied to me and trapped me,' Petra snapped at him. 'Yes, you are.'

Out of the corner of her eye she could see his mouth compress.

'We're married now, Petra, and—'

'For better, for worse… Don't remind me. We both know which it will be, don't we?'

'Look, it doesn't have to be like this, Petra. After all, we both already know that we have something in common, some shared ground…'

'And what ground would that be? The ground you're hoping to design another billion-pound complex on? Money! Is that all you can think about?'

Petra tensed as she felt his grip move from her elbow to her upper arm and tighten almost painfully on it as he bent his head and whispered with menacing silkiness in her ear, 'I would have thought that I had already proved to you that it is not. But if you wish me to show you again…'

Petra jerked away from him as though she had been scalded.

'If you ever, ever try to force me to…to accept you as my husband physically, then—'

'Force you?'

For a minute he looked as though she had somehow shocked him, but then his expression changed, hardening.

'Now you are being ridiculous,' he told her curtly. 'There

has never been any question of my doing any such thing. Even though…'

'Even though what?' Petra challenged him bitterly. 'Even though legally it is your right?'

She was almost beside herself with misery and anguish mixed to a toxic consistency by an over-active imagination and the fear that she was not as indifferent to him as she wanted to be.

Now that the ceremony was over she was face to face with the knowledge that tonight she would be his wife— his bride. He was a sensually passionate man; she already knew that! If he chose to consummate their marriage would she have the strength to reject and deny him?

'Rashid, your uncle has been looking for you…'

Petra released her breath in a sigh of relief as he moved away from her.

Several hours later, blank-eyed with exhaustion and misery, Petra stared bitterly in front of her, wishing she was any-where but where she was and anyone but who she was— or rather who she was now.

Her godfather had not been able to join them. No doubt he would save his celebrations until after the New Year and the announcement of his peerage, Petra reflected savagely.

Her marriage to Rashid had been trumpeted in the press as the romance of the year, but of course she knew better! She hated Rashid more than she had ever thought it possible for her to hate anyone, she decided wearily, and she knew she would never, ever forgive him for what he had done to her.

Finally the celebrations were drawing to a close. Finally her attendants were coming to carry her away to the suite that had been set aside for her to change out of her wedding dress and into her 'going-away' clothes.

'Where is Rashid taking you on honeymoon? Do you
know?' one of the girls, a married niece of her aunt, asked
Petra before shushing the knowing giggles of some of the
younger bridesmaids.

Petra was tempted to reply that she neither knew nor
cared, but good manners prevented her from doing so.

'I don't really know,' she replied instead.

'It's a secret. Oh, how romantic,' another of the girls
exclaimed enviously.

Yet another chimed in, more practically, 'But how did
you know what clothes to pack if you don't know where
you are going?'

'She's going on honeymoon, silly,' another one submitted. 'So clothes won't—'

'Stop it, all of you,' the oldest and most sensible of her
attendants instructed. 'You are supposed to be helping
Petra, not gossiping like schoolgirls. You must not worry.
A man as experienced as Rashid will know exactly what
to do!' she soothed Petra. 'I can remember how nervous I
was on my wedding night. I had no idea what to expect,
and I was terrified that my husband would not know what
I needed, but I should have had more trust in him…or
rather in my mother.' She grinned. 'She had ensured that I
had all the right clothes—although I suspect if it had been
left to Sayeed I might not.'

Clothes! She was talking about clothes! Petra didn't
know whether to laugh or cry!

At last it was over and she was ready, dressed in the
simple cream trouser suit she had bought in the exclusive
shopping centre nearby. The plain diamond ear studs which
had been her mother's, and which she had worn since her
death, had been removed from her ears and replaced by the
much larger pair which had been part of Rashid's wedding
present to her. She felt like ripping them out and destroying

them, but of course that wasn't possible, with her attendants exclaiming excitedly over the clarity and perfection of the stones, obviously chosen to complement the diamonds in her platinum engagement and wedding rings.

She had been misted with a fresh cloud of Rashid's perfume, and handed the minute scraps of silk and lace that her aunt was pleased to call underwear—Petra still couldn't believe that such minute scraps of fabric could cost so very, very much. Her manicure and pedicure had been checked by her eagle-eyed chief attendant, who seemed to believe that it would be a lifelong reflection on her if Petra was not handed over into the hands of her new husband looking anything less than immaculate. Now she was apparently ready to be handed into the care of her husband like a sweetmeat to be unwrapped and enjoyed—or discarded as he saw fit!

'Come—it is time. Rashid is waiting,' her chief attendant announced importantly.

As Petra looked towards the closed door to the suite the busy giggles fluttering around her died away.

'Be happy,' the chief attendant told her as she kissed her.

'May your life be full of the laughter of your children and the love of your husband,' the second whispered, as all the girls queued up to offer her their good wishes for her future and exchange shy embraces with her.

'May the nights of your marriage be filled with pleasure,' the boldest-eyed and most daring told her.

The noise from outside her suite was becoming deafening.

'If we do not open the door soon Rashid might break it down,' someone giggled, and there was an instant flurry of excited and delighted female panic as the door was pulled open and Petra was prodded and pushed through it.

The assembled wedding guests standing outside cheered

exuberantly when they saw her, but Petra barely noticed their enthusiasm. Across the small space that separated them her bitter gaze clashed with Rashid's.

Like her, he was dressed in Western-style clothes. Designers the world over would have paid a fortune to have Rashid wearing their logo, Petra decided with clinical detachment, refusing to allow her heartbeat to react to the casual togetherness of his appearance. Place him in any city in the world and he would immediately be recognised as a man of style and class, a man of wealth and knowledge. Wealthy, educated people like Rashid shared a common bond, no matter what their place of birth, Petra acknowledged distantly.

Silently he extended his hand towards her.

The crowd started to cheer. Briefly Petra hesitated, her glance going betrayingly to the windows, as though seeking freedom, but someone gave her a firm little push and her fingertips touched Rashid's hand and were swiftly enclosed by it.

With almost biblical immediacy, the crowd parted to allow them to pass through. The huge double doors to the private garden of the banqueting suite were flung open, and as they stepped out into the softness of the night perfectly timed fireworks exploded, sending sprays of brilliantly coloured stars showering earthwards.

At the same time they were deluged with handfuls of scented rose petals, and the air was filled with a pink-tinged cloud of strawberry scented *shisha* smoke. Doves swooped and flew, and a cloud of shimmering butterflies appeared as if by magic—music played, people laughed and called out good wishes to them, and Rashid drew her relentlessly towards the exit to the garden.

As he touched her arm and held her for one last second to face their audience, he whispered wryly in her ear, 'Your aunt wanted me to whisk you away on an Arab steed, complete with traditional Arabic trappings, but I managed to dissuade her.'

Caught off guard by the note of humour underlining his words, Petra turned automatically to look at him. 'You mean like a prince from an Arabian fairytale? Complete with medieval accoutrements including your falcon?'

'I suspect she would have wanted to pass on the falcon—for the sake of the doves—and I certainly would not have wanted to expose my prize birds to this fairground.'

As she looked at him Petra felt her heart suddenly miss not one beat but two.

As though a veil had abruptly lifted, giving her a clear view of something she had previously only perceived in a shadowy distorted fashion, she recognised an unwanted, unpalatable, unbearably painful truth!

In believing that logic, reality, anger and moral right were enough to destroy her unwanted love for Rashid she had deceived herself even more thoroughly and cruelly than Rashid himself could ever have done.

Had she married Rashid because secretly deep down inside she still wanted him? Still loved him? Petra was filled with self-contempt and loathing, her fiery pride hating the very idea!

She had believed that her most dangerous enemy lay outside the armed citadel of her heart, in the shape of Rashid himself, but she had been wrong. Her worst enemy lay within herself, within her own heart, in the form of her love for him.

But Rashid must never ever know that. She must forever be on her guard to protect herself and her emotions. She and they must become a fortress which Rashid must never be allowed to penetrate!

*   *   *

'Welcome to your new home!'

For the first time since they had left the hotel Rashid broke the silence between them. They had driven into the courtyard of the villa several seconds earlier, its creamy toned wall, warmed to gold by the discreet nightscape lighting. Her whole body rigid with the effort of maintaining the guard she was clinging to so desperately, Petra had discovered that her throat had locked so tensely that she couldn't even speak!

Once inside the villa she felt no more relaxed—quite the opposite.

'It's late, and it has been a very long day,' she heard Rashid saying calmly. 'I suggest that we both get a good night's sleep before you begin another round of hostilities. I have arranged for you to have your own suite of rooms. Not exactly the traditional way to conduct a wedding night, perhaps, but then it is not as though it would be our first time together.' Her gave a small dismissive shrug whilst Petra struggled to assimilate a feeling which was not entirely composed of relief! 'This has been a stressful time for you, and you need a little breathing space, I suspect, to accustom yourself to what is to be. Despite your comments earlier, I can assure you that there is no way I intend to…to force the issue between us, Petra!'

Petra stared at him. He sounded so controlled, so calm, so…so laid-back and casual almost. And as for his comment about arranging for her to have her own rooms—that was not at all what she had been expecting!

From the moment he had proposed formally to her this night had been at the back of Petra's mind. This moment when they would be alone as husband and wife. Fiercely she had told herself that no matter what kind of pressure he put on her to break down her resolve she would not allow him to touch her!

And yet now he was the one telling her that he did not want her!

A distinctly unpleasant mix of emotions filled her. Shock, disbelief, chagrin…and…

Disappointment? Most certainly not! Relief—that was what she felt. Yes, she was perhaps just a touch disappointed that he had stolen her thunder by not allowing her the satisfaction of being the one to tell him that she didn't want him. But at the end of the day what really mattered was that she was going to be free to sleep on her own…without him. Sleeping in her own bed and not his…just as though they were not married at all. And that was just what she wanted. Exactly what she wanted!

At last she was on her own. Which was just what she wanted. So why couldn't she go to sleep? Why was she lying here feeling so…lost and abandoned? So unwanted…and unloved and so hurt?

What was it that she longed for so much? Rashid? Blaize?

No! What she ached for, so much that it hurt, Petra acknowledged tormentedly as she burrowed into the emptiness of her huge bed, was to be able to trust the man she loved. Because without such trust, without being able to be open and honest with one another, how could two people possibly claim to share love?

CHAPTER TEN

A LITTLE apprehensively, Petra surveyed the other women crowding into the exclusive enclosure.

It was the start of the horse racing season and Petra suspected that by now, after over a month of marriage, she ought to be familiar with the high-octane and very glamorous nature of the social events to which her position as Rashid's wife gave her an entrée.

In the short time they had been married they had already had the tennis championships, and a celebrity golf tournament, in addition to a whole host of business events sponsored by the Royal Family in which Rashid, as one of their most favoured architects and a business partner, had played a high-profile role.

And now, within a few days, it would be the most prestigious event of the Zuran social calendar—the Zuran Cup, the world's most glamorous horse race.

Horses, trainers, jockeys, owners and their elegant wives had been pouring into Zuran all month—the whole city was in a state of excited expectancy over the race and its eventual winner.

Rashid was entering his own horse, an American-bred and Irish-trained three-year-old stabled at his training yard close to the racecourse. Along with a mere handful of other specially favoured owners, Rashid was permitted to use the actual racecourse itself for training purposes.

Petra and Rashid were due to entertain a group of businessmen and diplomats and their partners from America and Europe, and for the duration of Race Week they would be staying at the hotel complex with their guests.

Unlike some of the other wives, Petra had not found it necessary to fly to Paris or Milan to order a series of one-off couture outfits for the event—although she had taken her aunt's advice and been to see a visiting top milliner to ensure that her hat for the occasion was 'special' enough for her position as the wife of an owner of one of the competing horses.

At the breathtakingly stunning villa he had designed and had built, in its equally breathtaking setting of his private oasis, they had entertained a variety of prominent politicians, sportsmen and women and businessmen from all over the world, including the UK, and never once on any of those occasions had Rashid faltered in enacting his own chosen role of devoted husband.

But in private things were very different. Rashid kept to his own suite of rooms in the villa, as she did hers, and when they were not entertaining or being entertained Petra hardly saw him.

He was either working, visiting various projects he was involved in virtually all over the world or, when he was at home, he would be down in the stables where he kept the racehorses he had in training, discussing their progress with his racing manager.

Of course Petra had commitments of her own. She had been invited to join the Zuran Ladies Club, headed by Her Highness—the club's remit being to provide a common ground for the exchange of ideas between women belonging to different nationalities and cultures. She had gone to women's lunches and fund-raising events, and an embryo friendship was developing between her and her most senior wedding attendant—a relative of her aunt by marriage. But these were the outer layers of her married life.

The inner ones were very different and very painful.

Common sense told her that the discovery she had not conceived Rashid's child should have been greeted with relief. Instead she had spent the night silently weeping with anguished disappointment. His child would at least have been something of him she would have been allowed to publicly love.

And that was the private pain which was slowly destroying her.

Outwardly, in the eyes of other people, she must seem as though she had everything anyone could possibly want, Petra reflected as she checked her appearance in her bedroom mirror.

Rashid, who was currently away on business and was not due to return for another two days, had kept his promise not to touch her. Indeed, he quite obviously found it a very easy promise to keep; his relaxed calm politeness whenever they were together made her grit her teeth together against the fury of physical and emotional confusion she herself was enduring.

How was it possible for her to want him so much when he quite obviously did not want her? She lay in bed at night aching for him. Longing for him, thinking about him—fantasising about him, if she was honest—and then in the morning was filled with such a sense of self-revulsion and despair at her own lack of self-control that she despised herself even more than she did him.

He treated her as distantly as though she were merely a visiting house guest—an outsider to his world and life to whom he was obliged to be polite. She had absolutely no idea what he might be thinking or feeling about their marriage, or about her, and that further intensified her sense of loneliness and frustration. It was not natural to live in the way they were doing, and her body, her mind, her heart, her spirit rebelled against it.

She wanted to share her life and herself fully with the man she loved, but how could she do that when that man was Rashid, a man who did not love her in return? A man she could not trust!

She paused in the process of packing her clothes for their Race Week stay in the hotel complex, a tiny, fine tremble of sensation electrifying her at the thought of seeing Rashid. Angrily she dismissed it. She reminded herself firmly instead that she was due to visit the racecourse stables to discuss with Rashid's trainer what arrangements needed to be made with regard to guests visiting the stables to view the horses.

Already, although they were still in March, the temperature had climbed well into the high thirties, and Petra dressed accordingly, in cotton jeans and a long sleeved tee shirt, plus a hat to protect her head from the sun.

The young man Rashid had appointed as her driver smiled happily at her as he opened the car door for her.

Petra had timed her visit to coincide with the end of the morning exercise session, and when she walked into the yard it was bustling with activity as the newly exercised horses were returned to their stables.

Rashid's manager and trainer were standing together on the far side of the stable yard talking to one another as Petra walked in. Several other groups of people were in the stable yard, including two small dark-haired children.

Smiling at them, Petra started to make her way towards Rashid's manager and trainer, but as she did so she saw one of the children suddenly dart across the yard, right into the path of the highly strung, nervously sweating young horse being led across the yard by his handler.

As the horse reared up Petra reacted instinctively, making a grab for the child and snatching him from beneath the horse's hooves.

She could hear the uproar going on all around her; the shrill squeal of fear from the horse and the even shriller scream of panic from the child, the groom's anxious voice, the voices of the onlookers, and then the breath was driven out of her lungs as the world exploded in an agonising red mist of searing pain followed by a terrifying sensation of whirling darkness as she hit the ground.

Blearily Petra opened her eyes.

'Ah, good, you've finally come round properly.'

A uniformed nurse smiled at her. Weakly Petra began to move, and then winced as she felt the pain in her shoulder.

'Don't worry, it isn't serious. Just a very nasty bruise, that's all,' the nurse comforted her cheerfully. 'You were lucky, though, and the little boy you rescued was even luckier.'

The child! Petra sat up anxiously and then gasped as pain ripped through her shoulder.

'Are you sure he's okay?' she pressed the nurse.

'He's fine—in fact I think his father is in a worse state of shock than he was. They are related to the Royal Family, you know. Cousins, I think. The father couldn't sing your praises highly enough. He is convinced that if you hadn't acted so promptly the horse might have killed his son.'

'It wasn't the horse's fault!' Petra protested. 'The yard was busy, and he was obviously nervous... Ouch!' She winced as the nurse readjusted the strapping holding the protective pad in place against her skin.

'Don't worry, I'm just checking to see if you've stopped bleeding.'

'Bleeding?' Petra frowned.

'The horse's shoe caught your shoulderblade, and as well

as inflicting a wonderful-looking bruise it's also broken the skin. It looks fine now, though.'

'Good—in that case, I can get dressed and go home,' Petra said.

'Not until the doctor has given you the all-clear,' the nurse warned her.

Half an hour later Petra was sitting fully dressed on the side of her bed, frowning mutinously at the young doctor confronting her.

'Look, I can't stay in overnight,' she told him firmly. 'We're less than a week away from Race Week, and I've got a hundred things I have to do. You've said yourself that you're ninety-nine per cent sure that I don't have concussion, and—'

'I would still prefer you to stay in overnight, just to be on the safe side,' the doctor was telling her insistently.

Petra shook her head.

'There really isn't any need. I promise you I feel fine.'

'We should at least alert your husband to what has happened,' the doctor persisted.

Rashid. Petra tensed. Right now he was in London, overseeing some problem with the alterations to the hotel which the Royal Family had just acquired to add to their portfolio of hotel properties. He wasn't due back for another two days, and she could just imagine how he was going to feel if he was dragged back on account of a wife who emotionally meant nothing whatsoever to him at all!

Determinedly she set about convincing the young doctor that there was no reason why Rashid should be unnecessarily alarmed about a mere minor accident, when he would be home within a couple of days anyway, and to Petra's relief he seemed to accept her argument.

When it came to allowing her to go home, though, he

was harder to persuade, but in the end he gave in and said that provided she was not going to be left on her own, and that there was someone there to keep an eye on her, he would agree to discharge her.

Assuring him that there was, Petra held her breath whilst he checked her bruised shoulder, and then wrote her a prescription for some painkillers, before finally agreeing to her discharge.

An hour later she was on her way home, gritting her teeth against the unexpectedly intense pain in her shoulder as she was driven slowly and carefully back to the villa by her very protective and anxious young driver.

Once there, she was fussed over by Rashid's staff to an extent that made her grit her teeth a little and insist that they stop treating her as though she was a fragile piece of china.

Within an hour of her return she had received so many concerned telephone calls that she was refusing to take any more, and the largest reception room of the villa was filled with floral tributes—including an enormous display from the Royal Family, thanking her for rescuing one of their family.

Ignoring the dull, nagging ache which even the strong painkillers she had been given at the hospital had not totally suppressed, Petra went into the room she used as her office and started to go through the sample menus submitted to her by the hotel's senior chef.

Their guests would be dining in one of the hotel's private dining rooms, and Petra worked into the evening, meticulously checking the profiles she had been given of their guests against the chef's suggested menus, stopping only to eat the light meal which Rashid's housekeeper brought her and to reassure her that she was feeling completely fine apart from having an aching shoulder. At midnight Petra decided that she had had enough and tidied away her papers before making her way to her suite.

The live-in staff had their own quarters, separate from the main villa. Quite what the housekeeper thought of a newly married couple who slept apart Petra had no idea, but the housekeeper had confided to her that Rashid had had her suite of rooms completely redecorated prior to their marriage, even though the villa was brand-new and the rooms had previously been unoccupied.

The villa embraced the best of both Eastern and Western cultures, and had a clean, almost minimalistic look that reminded her of certain exclusive West Coast American homes belonging to friends of her parents, where modern simplicity was broken up and softened by the intriguing addition of single antique pieces. In the case of Rashid's villa, there was an underlying sense of traditional Moorish décor which really appealed to Petra's senses. Even the colours he had chosen were sympathetic to the eye and the landscape: pale sands, soft terracottas, a delicate watery blue-green here and there to break up the neutral natural colours.

Stunning sculptures and pieces of artwork made subtle statements about Rashid's wealth and taste, fabrics made to delight the touch as well as the eye softened any starkness—and yet the villa felt alien and unwelcoming to Petra.

Despite its elegance and comfort, something essential was missing from it. It was a house empty of love, with no sense of being a home, of having a heart! To Petra, acutely sensitive about such things, it lacked that aura of being a place where people who loved one another lived.

She winced a little as she removed the bandage from her back and shoulder, but when she peered over her shoulder to study her reflection in the mirror in her bathroom she was relieved to see that, despite the livid bruising swelling her skin, the raw scrape on her flesh looked clean and had stopped bleeding. As she stood beneath the warm spray of a shower that was large enough for two people to share with comfort she winced a little with pain. She would have some discomfort for some days to come, the doctor had warned her.

It was the horse she felt most sorry for, Petra decided ruefully a little later as she discarded her wrap and slid naked into her bed. The poor animal had been nervous enough before the incident.

Her bed felt deliciously cool. It had been made up with clean, immaculate linen sheets that day. Forlornly Petra turned onto her side. The bed was huge, making her feel acutely conscious of the fact that, despite her marriage, she was still living the life of a partnerless woman. A woman whose husband did not want her, did not desire her, did not love her. Whilst she…

Whilst she had not gone one single night since her marriage without longing for Rashid to be here with her, without giving in to the hopeless, helpless temptation to recreate those hours she had spent in his arms at the oasis. Tiredly Petra closed her eyes against the slow fall of threatening tears.

Abruptly Petra opened her eyes, wincing as she tried to move her painfully stiff shoulder.

'Petra, are you all right?'

She gave a small gasp of shock as she stared into the darkness to where Rashid was sitting beside the bed.

'Rashid!'

Immediately she struggled to sit up, ignoring the dull nagging ache from her shoulder as she clutched the bedclothes to her body, her heart thudding furiously.

'You weren't supposed to be coming back yet! What are you doing here?'

'What do you think I'm doing here?' he answered her grimly. 'I received a message to say that you had been involved in an accident and that there were grave concerns that you could be suffering from concussion. Naturally I caught the first flight back that I could.'

'You didn't need to do that.' Petra protested. 'I'm perfectly all right…apart from a stiff shoulder,' she added ruefully.

Whilst she had been speaking Rashid had switched on the lamp at the side of her bed.

Petra sucked in her breath as she saw him properly for the first time. She had never seen him looking so formidably severe, harsh lines etched from his nose to his mouth, his expression wintry and bleak.

'I'm sorry that you had to come back—' she began.

'What on earth were you thinking about?' Rashid overrode her apology. 'Is marriage to me really so unbearable that you prefer to throw yourself under the hooves of a horse and be trampled to death?'

Petra stared at him, stunned by the bleak bitterness in his voice.

'It wasn't like that,' she protested. 'There was a child…I simply acted instinctively, as anyone would have done.'

His frown deepened.

'I hadn't heard about a child, only that there had nearly been a terrible tragedy and that you had insisted on leaving the hospital even though there was concern that you might not be well enough to do so.'

'I have a bruised shoulder, that is all.' Petra told, him making light of her injury. The truth was that she was far more interested in discovering why the thought of her being injured had brought him all the way home from London than in discussing her very minor bruises with him.

'When I spoke to the hospital the doctor said that he was concerned there was a risk that you might experience concussion.'

'You came back because of that?' Petra was openly incredulous.

'He warned you that you should not be on your own,' Rashid told her grimly.

'He admitted that the risk was minimal and that he was virtually one hundred per cent sure that I would be okay. And anyway I'm not on my own—the staff—' Petra began.

'Are not here to keep a proper watch over you,' Rashid interrupted her. 'But I am.'

As he spoke he moved, and Petra saw how tired he looked.

'Rashid, I'm fine,' she told him. 'Look, why don't you go to bed and—'

'I'm staying right here,' he told her flatly.

Petra sighed. 'I promise you, there is no need. If I hadn't felt completely well I would not have come back to the villa.'

'That's fine. But, like I just said, until I'm convinced that you're okay I'm staying here,' Rashid reiterated.

Petra sighed again, hunching her uninjured shoulder defensively as she told him tiredly, 'Have it your own way, Rashid, but honestly there's no need for you to stay.'

As he reached out to switch off the light Rashid instructed her flatly, 'Go back to sleep.'

Quietly Petra moved her head. She could hear Rashid breathing, but she couldn't see him sitting in the chair beside her bed. And then, as she looked across the bed, she saw him.

He was lying on his back on the bed beside her fast asleep.

The moon was up and full, casting a soft silvery light through the gauzy curtains of her room. Propping herself up on one elbow, she studied Rashid's sleeping form. Watching him sleep and seeing him so vulnerable sent a huge wave of tenderness aching through her.

At some stage he had unfastened the shirt he had been wearing and the white fabric was a pale blur against the darkness of his skin. There was evidence of his long day in the dark shadow bearding his jaw, and her muscles tensed a little in female response to such evidence of his maleness. Before she could stop herself she was reaching out to touch his jaw experimentally with her fingertips, and she felt her tenderness give way to sharply spiked desire.

As her fingers started to tremble she snatched them away, curling them into a fist and imprisoning them with her other hand. But, although she had managed to stop herself from touching him, she couldn't stop herself from looking at him, her love-hungry gaze fastening greedily on his mouth, his throat, the exposed flesh of his torso.

Now it wasn't just her fingers that were trembling, it was her whole body! She could feel the hot urgency of her own desire seeping into every nerve-ending—seeping, flowing, flooding through her until it swamped her completely.

Rashid! Tormentedly she mouthed his name, and then jumped back as he stirred in his sleep, his eyes starting to open.

By the time he had fully opened them she had retreated to her own side of the bed and was lying defensively still as she tried to feign sleep.

'Petra?' She heard the anxiety in his sleep-thickened voice as he leaned towards her. His hand touched her throat, checking her pulse, monitoring its frantic race.

'Petra, wake up,' he was commanding her.

'Rashid, it's all right—I do not have concussion,' she told him briefly, guessing what he was thinking, turning her head to look at him and trying to shrug off his hand as she did so.

But suddenly he had gone completely still, his hand lying against her throat with heavy immobility. His gaze was fixed on her breasts, naked and exposed by her inadvertent negligence in failing to pull the covers up over her body.

She knew immediately and instinctively that he wanted her, and she knew just as instinctively that he would keep to the promise he had made her on the day of their wedding not to force himself on her.

All she needed to do was to reach for her covers and turn away from him. If that was what she wanted...

And if it wasn't? Hardly daring to acknowledge what was going through her mind, Petra held his gaze. She could feel the longing and need curling through her, gaining force and power, filling her until her whole body felt like a highly tuned instrument of desire, openly aching for his touch. She could feel her breasts swell and lift, her nipples tighten and ache, her belly sink in slightly against the desire flooding her sex.

Lifting her hand, she curled her fingers around his forearm, slowly caressing it, her eyes wide open as she gazed up into his.

She could feel the open tremor of his body at her touch, see the way he was fighting to draw extra air into his lungs. What was he thinking? Feeling? A fierce surge of excitement and power filled her as she read the answer in the hot gleam of his eyes and the immediate response of his body!

'Hold me, Rashid,' she commanded him boldly, shuddering violently as he did so, tightening his arms around her so that they were body to body, so that she could feel the heavy, exciting thud of his heart.

'Love me!' she whispered passionately against his hot skin, knowing that he could not hear the betraying words, only feel the warmth of her breath.

She heard—and felt—the low growl of sound he made deep in his throat! Frustration? Longing?

Her body responded to it immediately, her lips parting eagerly for the savage sweet pleasure of his kiss.

Instantly she was plunged into a spiral of aching need, a swift descent into the thick velvet heat of her own most primitive longings. Her hand pressed to the back of Rashid's head, she urged him to increase the pressure of his mouth against her own, until all rational thought was suspended beneath its bruisingly passionate heat.

Petra knew that she should have been horrified by and contemptuous of her own behaviour, that she should have totally resisted her own desire. But instead she could feel her heart turning over inside her chest and then slamming heavily into her ribs as shockingly elemental and savage emotions exploded into life inside her. She had wanted this so much, she recognised dizzily. She had wanted, needed him so much!

'Petra,' Rashid groaned against her mouth. 'This isn't…'

He moved, his hand accidentally brushing against her breast, and Petra froze. In the darkness she could feel his gaze searching the distance between them, penetrating the moon-silvered darkness and then fixing unerringly on the betraying peak of her nipple, where it pouted with deliberate invitation so dangerously close to his stilled hand.

'Petra?' This time when he said her name it held a different note, a male huskiness and timbre that her sensitive female ears interpreted as an open acknowledgement of his desire for her.

She could feel the power that his desire for her gave her. She was all Eve, a wanton temptress, holding her breath whilst she willed him to reach out to her, for her, already knowing the pleasure he would give her.

Very slowly his hand moved back towards her breast. Petra exhaled shakily, and then closed her eyes as he stroked her skin with the lightest of touches—so light that it was little more than a breath, and yet so sensual that her whole breast seemed to swell and yearn towards him.

'Petra.'

This time her name was muffled beneath the slow, lingering kisses he was threading around the base of her throat like a necklace. A necklace that reached down between her breasts and was then strung from the upper curve of one breast to the other.

At some stage Petra had started to tremble. Tiny little inner secret tremors at first, but by the time Rashid was cupping one breast in his hand, laving the delighted pink-flushed crest of the other with his tongue, they had turned into galvanic shudders of uncontrollable mute delight. And then not so mute, when Petra was forced to bite down hard on her bottom lip to prevent herself from crying out aloud.

When Rashid saw what she was doing he lifted his mouth from her nipple to watch her, and then slid his finger into her mouth, freeing her bottom lip whilst he told her thickly, 'Taste me instead, Petra!'

Her whole body reacted to his words, swept with a molten need that burned openly in her eyes.

'Yes! *Yes!*' he told her savagely, even though she had said nothing, spoken no question. But Petra knew that he had heard the silent hungry longing of her body, seen her need for him in her eyes.

'Yes,' he repeated more softly. 'Whatever... However...

Every which way you want, Petra. Every way, until you beg me to end our mutual torment.'

As he was speaking he was kissing her. Tiny slow kisses that were a torment in themselves as his hands shaped her body, effortlessly drawing from it everything that it ached so wantonly to give him and everything that she herself did not.

Her need, herself, her life. Her love...

She cried out in shocked denial under the touch of his tongue against her sex, and then cried out again in a low, guttural woman's cry of acknowledgement of the pleasure he was showing her. But when he moaned in response, and placed her hand on his body, her reaction caused him to lift his head and demand rawly, 'Did you think you are the only one to have pleasure in what I'm doing, in the feel of you, the heat of you, the taste of you? I've hungered for you like this Petra, for this intimacy with you...this possession of you.'

As he stopped speaking he turned his head and kissed the inside of her thigh. Petra trembled and then moaned as he kissed her again, more intimately. Her longing for his physical possession of her overwhelmed every other emotion she felt surging through her in an unstoppable, undammable torrent.

Petra didn't know if she had actually reached for Rashid or if he had simply known how she felt, how she ached...how she loved and needed. But suddenly he was there, where she most wanted him to be. Where she most needed him to be. Filling her with surge after powerful surge of exquisite sensation and unparalleled ecstasy.

She wanted it to never end. And yet she knew she would die if she did not reach the summit, the frantic crescendo of her completion. She thought she already knew the sensation, the pleasure, the fulfilment, but when the spasms began and she felt the hot sweet thickness of Rashid's own release within her she knew that all she had known had been a pale remembered shadow of real pleasure.

CHAPTER ELEVEN

'PETRA, are you sure you are all right?'

'Grandfather, I am fine,' Petra fibbed as she turned away from him to prevent him from seeing her tears.

He had arrived unexpectedly that morning, just after Rashid had left to visit the stables, anxious to find out how Petra was for himself.

'No, you aren't,' he insisted, coming up to her and turning her towards him. 'You are crying. What's wrong?' he asked sternly.

Petra bit her lip. She still felt seared, scorched, shamed by her memories of the previous night! And there was no point in her trying to mentally blame Rashid! She had been the one to instigate things...even if he had carried them...and her...to a point...place...she had never imagined existed!

She was furious with herself for her weakness, unable to accept her own behaviour. How could she have been so weak-willed as to give in to temptation? Why couldn't she make herself stop loving him? Especially when she knew there was no future for them; when she knew she couldn't trust him.

He didn't love her. He might have returned early from his business trip. He might have made love with her last night...he might even have stayed with her until she had fallen asleep. But he had never made any attempt to talk to her, to tell her...

To tell her what? That he loved her? But she already

knew that he did not, didn't she? She already knew that he had been forced to marry her!

They were trapped in a marriage which could only cause them both misery. And now, thanks to her behaviour last night, there could be additional complications. What if this time she *had* conceived his baby?

'You are not happy,' her grandfather was persisting. 'You are too thin...too pale. This was not what I expected when you and Rashid married. You are so obviously suited to one another in so many ways.' He started to frown.

Petra stared at him. Suited to one another! How could he think that?

'In your eyes, perhaps,' she told him unhappily. 'But no...! We should never have married. Rashid feels nothing for me. He doesn't love me and...I—'

'Petra, what nonsense is this?' her grandfather demanded immediately. 'Of course Rashid loves you! That has never been in any doubt! It is quite obvious how he feels about you from the way he talks about you, from the way he has behaved towards you.'

'No!' Petra stopped him in disbelief 'You're wrong! How can you say that he loves me? The only reason Rashid married me is because he...he had to!'

'Had to?' To Petra's consternation her grandfather actually laughed. 'What on earth gave you that idea? It was most certainly not the case at all!'

He gave her a wry look. 'It is, of course, true that the pair of you would logically be expected to marry, having spent so much time together unchaperoned, but I can assure you that there was no obligation for Rashid to marry you other than his own desire to do so! And I can also tell you that that desire sprang entirely from his love for you!'

Her grandfather shook his head. 'And, besides, Rashid would never have allowed himself to be involved in such a potentially compromising situation if he had not been passionately in love with you!'

Her grandfather spoke with such conviction that Petra was dumbfounded.

'There is only one reason Rashid married you, Petra,' he repeated. 'And that is quite simply that he loves you.'

'If that is true then why has he never told me so himself?' Petra asked emotionally, reluctant to allow herself to trust what she was hearing.

'Have you told him of your love for him?' her grandfather challenged her gently.

Biting her lip, Petra had to confess that she had not.

'But you do love him?' her grandfather persisted.

Petra could not bring herself to reply. She could see that her grandfather was frowning.

'If I have misjudged your feelings, Petra, then you must say so,' she heard him telling her with gentle firmness. 'Much as I like and respect Rashid, you are my granddaughter. If you have discovered that you do not love him, if you are in any way unhappy, then you can come home with me now and I shall speak to Rashid if you wish.'

Petra's eyes darkened with emotion.

'I feel so confused. There is so much I...I believed...I thought...' She stopped and took a deep breath. 'I thought that Rashid married me because of the financial benefits our marriage would bring him,' she confessed, blurting out her despair.

'The financial benefits?' Her grandfather looked bemused. 'Petra—' he began, but Petra stopped him, rushing on fiercely.

'Saud told me everything, Grandfather. You mustn't be cross with him. He didn't realise that I didn't know there was a...a plan to have me marry Rashid—whether I wanted to or not! Saud hero-worships him so much that he thought

I would be pleased…thrilled. I know all about…everything. Even my godfather seemed to think it was a good idea. So much so that he abandoned me here without my passport so that I couldn't leave…'

'Petra, Petra. My dear child. Please! You are distressing yourself so unnecessarily!'

Petra fell silent as she heard the pain in her grandfather's voice. 'Come and sit down here beside me,' he commanded her gently.

A little reluctantly she did so.

'You are right in thinking there was a suggestion that you and Rashid should meet one another, and that it was felt that…that you had a great deal in common—but you must understand that a suggestion was all it was, made more in jest than anything else. Saud obviously eaves-dropped on that conversation and leapt to incorrect assumptions…' He frowned. 'You may be sure that I shall have some strong words to say to him about his behaviour and his actions in passing on his totally unfounded assumptions to you. As you say, he greatly admires Rashid… But I can assure you that Rashid immediately insisted that what was being suggested was totally out of the question. Rashid has far too much pride, too much of the same spirit I can see so clearly in you, to ever allow anyone else to make that kind of decision for him,' he told her ruefully.

'As for your godfather.' He gave a small rueful shrug. 'He is a statesman and a diplomat—who knows what such men think? Intrigue is their bread and meat. If it does not exist then they create it!'

Petra had to acknowledge that there was some truth in his assessment of her godfather, even if his description of him leaned towards the slightly over-cynical.

Shaking his head, he continued, 'After losing Mija there was no way I would ever want to repeat the mistake I made with her. There was only one reason I wanted you to come to Zuran, Petra, and that is because you are my grandchild and because I longed so much to see you!'

'Grandfather, I know that you and Rashid are in business together,' Petra persisted. 'And that he is dependent on the patronage of the Royal Family! I know that there were diplomatic reasons…'

Petra stared at her grandfather as he started to laugh.

'Why are you laughing?' she demanded, offended.

'Petra, Rashid is a millionaire many times over in his own right, from the inheritance left to him by his father. We do have business interests in common, yes—and indeed the Royal Family are great admirers of his work—but Rashid is dependent on no one's patronage!'

Shaking his head, he added huskily, 'Petra, I did your mother a terrible wrong, but the price I paid is one I shall pay to the end of my days. There is never a sunrise when I do not think of your mother, nor a sunset when I do not mourn her loss.'

Petra blinked, her eyes wet with fresh tears. Instinctively she knew that her grandfather was telling the truth.

'Are you still feeling unhappy? Do you want to come home with me now?' he asked her. 'I shall speak with Rashid for you, if you wish. The decision is yours, but it seems to me that it would be a pity if two such well-matched people should lose one another through a simple matter of pride, and lack of communication and trust.'

Her grandfather made it all sound so easy!

'No… No, I do not wish you to speak to Rashid,' she answered him.

'I…I…can do that myself…'

The smile he was giving her made her colour self-consciously.

'It isn't for me to interfere, but you are my granddaughter,' he told her gently. 'It seems to me that you and Rashid are very well suited. You are both strong-minded, you are both proud, you share a spirit of independence; these are all good things, but sometimes such virtues can lead to a little too much self-sufficiency—claimed not because that is what a person necessarily wants but because they believe it is what they have to have in order to protect themselves. I think that both you and Rashid are perhaps afraid to admit your great love for one another because you fear the other will think you weak and in need.'

His intuitive reading of her most private and hidden feelings astonished Petra.

Part of the reason she had fought so hard to resist her love for Rashid *had* been because she feared its intensity. Could it be true, as her grandfather had implied, that Rashid felt exactly the same?

She was, she recognised, still trying to come to terms with the fact that she had made such an error of judgement in assuming why he had married her. But he had made no attempt to defend himself to her, had he? Out of pride? Or because he didn't really care what she thought? And he had deceived her about who he really was!

'Sometimes in life we are tested where we are most vulnerable. There are many ways of being strong, many reasons for being proud,' her grandfather was continuing gently. 'Only you can decide whether or not your love for Rashid is worth fighting for, Petra—whether it means enough to you for you to take the risk of reaching out to him, openly and honestly. Rashid has already taken that risk by marrying you. It is his way of saying how much he wants to be with you. Remember he has married you in free will and of his own choice. Perhaps it is now time for you to take your risk!'

Silently Petra absorbed his words. He had given her an

insight into the workings of Rashid's mind and heart that she had not previously contemplated, and the possibilities springing to life from that insight were giving her an entrancing, an intoxicating, an impossible to resist picture of what they could share together.

'I have additionally been instructed to give this to you,' her grandfather continued, changing the subject. He handed her a beautifully decorated piece of rolled parchment and a flat oblong package.

Petra frowned. 'What is it?'

'Open it and see,' he said with a smile.

Hesitantly Petra did so, her glance skimming the letter written on the parchment and then studying it more slowly a second time, before she turned to the package and quickly unfastened it.

'It's a letter from the father of the little boy—the one at the stables,' she told her grandfather. 'He has written to thank me and he has…' Her voice tailed away and she gave a small gasp as she studied the contents of the package.

'It's ownership papers for a…a horse…a yearling…'

'Bred out of the Royal stables,' her grandfather supplied for her. 'They are very grateful to you for what you did, Petra. You saved the life of a very precious child…and at no small risk to your own.'

'But a horse!' Petra was overwhelmed.

'Not just a horse,' her grandfather corrected her with a smile. 'But a yearling whose breeding means that he may one day earn you, his owner, the Zuran Cup!'

From the balcony of the Presidential Suite Petra could see down to the beach. Race Week and all its excitement and busyness was over. She and Rashid had said goodbye to their last guests and in the morning they were due to leave the hotel for the villa.

Rashid's horse had come in a very respectable fourth, and Petra's grandfather had teased him that he might soon find himself in the position of having his wife's horse competing with his own.

There had been no opportunity for them to be on their own together since the night Rashid had made love to her at the villa, or for Petra to raise the subject she was desperately anxious to talk to him about.

According to her grandfather, Rashid loved her!

On a sudden impulse Petra left the suite and hurried towards the lift.

It was already almost dusk, the sun loungers around the pool empty, the beach deserted apart from one lone figure collecting the discarded windsurfers.

For a second his unexpected appearance checked Petra, and then she took a deep breath. She had initially intended to come down here merely to think, but perhaps fate had decided to take a hand in events.

The sand muffled her footsteps, but even so something must have alerted Rashid to her presence because he turned round to watch her in silence.

His formal clothes had been discarded and he was wearing a tee shirt and a pair of jeans.

Trying to control her nervousness, Petra walked up to him. His silence unnerved her, and she moistened her lips with the tip of her tongue, her face flushing as his gaze trapped the small betraying movement.

'I...I...have a proposition I want to put to you,' she told him, superstitiously crossing her fingers behind her back as she spoke.

How was he going to react? Was he going to walk away? Was he going to ignore her? Was he going to listen to her? Petra knew which she wanted him to do!

'A proposition?'

Well, at least he was responding to her, even if she could hear a grim note of cynicism in his voice.

'What kind of proposition?'

'I have a problem and I think you could be the very person to help me,' she said.

It was a relief that it was now fully dusk and he couldn't see her face—although she suspected that he must be able to hear the anxiety and uncertainty in her voice. If she had felt nervous the first time she had propositioned him then she felt a hundred—no, a thousand times more so now. Then all that had been at stake had been her freedom; now it was her whole life...her love...everything!

'I need you to help me find out if the man I love loves me. Until today I believed that he didn't, but now it seems I might have been wrong.'

'The man you love?' he questioned, and there was a new note in his voice that sent Petra's pulses racing.

'Yes. I love him so much that I'm almost afraid to admit just how much—even to myself, never mind to him—and I thought...'

'Yes?'

He had moved so swiftly and silently, and she had been so engrossed in her own anxiety, that his sudden proximity to her caught her off-guard.

'I thought you might be able to show me a way to show him just how I feel...' she said huskily.

'Oh, you did, did you? What inducement exactly were you planning to offer me in return for my co-operation?'

There was a distinct huskiness in his voice now, and Petra allowed herself to relax just a little.

'Oh...' She pretended to consider. 'I was rather thinking in terms of...er...payment in kind...'

'Uh-huh...'

Uh-huh. Was that going to be his only response? Nothing

more? Nothing more positive? More encouraging? Fresh uncertainty gripped her.

'If you aren't interested—' she began.

'Did I say that?' He was standing even closer to her now.

'No,' she admitted. 'But...'

'If you really wanted to prove to him that you do love him, I think a good place to start would be right here,' she heard him murmur. 'Right here, in his arms, like this...'

His arms were closing round her, holding her tight. Relief melted the tension from her bones.

'Like this?'

Was that thrilled little squeak really her voice?

'Uh-huh. And then you might show him that you liked being here by putting your arms around his neck, looking up in his eyes and...'

'Like this, you mean?' Petra whispered.

'Sort of... You're on the right track—but it would be even better if you did this!' Rashid told her, showing her what he meant as he brushed her lips with his own.

'Mmm... But what if I want to kiss him properly?' Petra asked him.

'Well, then I think you should go right ahead,' Rashid replied. 'But I ought to warn you that if you do that, he could very well want to...'

Sometimes actions could speak far more informatively than words, Petra decided dizzily as she daringly silenced Rashid's soft-voiced instructions with the loving pressure of her mouth against his.

It was a long, long time before either of them wanted to speak again, but when they had finally managed to stop kissing one another Rashid told her masterfully, 'I think our negotiations might be better conducted somewhere more...private.'

'Oh?' Petra gave him a mischievous look. 'Have you anywhere specific in mind? Only I am staying at the hotel.'

'What I have in mind,' Rashid responded softly, with an erotic undertone to his voice that made her heart dance in excited anticipation, 'is a very large bed, in a room that is preferably soundproofed so that no one can hear your cries of pleasure other than me…'

Since he was threading each word on a necklace of kisses round her throat, in between teasing her lips with the briefest of sensual contacts with his mouth, Petra was not really able to focus on too many specifics—although the words 'bed' and 'pleasure' did manage to penetrate her dizzying mist of euphoria.

As he kissed his way up the side of her neck and nibbled on her earlobe she demanded huskily, 'So it is true, then— you do love me?'

So abruptly that it shocked her, Rashid released her. For a moment Petra went icy cold with fear, but then she saw the expression in his eyes.

'I fell in love with you here on this beach, the evening you propositioned me,' Rashid told her quietly. 'Up until then you had just been a name I had heard mentioned in connection with your grandfather—someone who shared a similar parental background to my own, yes, but there are many, many offspring of mixed marriages living here.' He gave a small dismissive shrug. 'And then you accosted me here, and told me your wild tale of believing you were about to be forced into marriage to a man I admit even I was beginning to despise after I had listened to your description of him! And I thought that Saud liked me!' he commented drolly.

Petra had the grace to give him an abashed look.

'My grandfather told me that I'd got it all wrong, and that Saud had misunderstood what he had overheard!'

'A passing comment, between business partners, that was never intended to be taken seriously. Knowing how concerned your family was about your grandfather's health, and the effect your visit might have on it, I volunteered to show you something of the complex. But never for one moment did I intend to do so with a view to seeing if you might be a suitable wife!'

'Did you really fall in love with me that night?' Petra couldn't resist asking him.

'When I asked you what kind of man you wanted, and you told me…' He paused and looked away from her, before looking back again. 'I am a very wealthy man, Petra, and naturally I have been pursued by the kind of woman who sees a man only in terms of the financial benefits she can gain from him. When you spoke so passionately of your feelings and your beliefs, your hopes and desires for the way you wanted your life and your love to be, they so closely mirrored my own that I knew I could not let you walk away from me. And then I kissed you.'

'And you knew then?'

Petra knew that her voice was trembling, and that Rashid would be able to hear quite clearly the joy and incredulity in it, but now she felt no need to hide her feelings or to feel ashamed of them.

'Yes,' Rashid acknowledged simply.

'I knew then, and I was determined to court you…and woo you…but unfortunately I hadn't reckoned on your stubborn determination not to fall in love with the man you believed me to be. I was beginning to panic. I was afraid that I might lose you. And then you found out who I was and I thought I *had* lost you. I wasn't going to allow that to happen. Not when I knew just how good things could be for us.'

Petra gave him a wry look. 'So you had made up your mind that I loved you, had you?'

'Quite simply I could not bear to think of how my life would be if you didn't!'

His admission dissolved any potential suspicion of arrogance or lack of respect for her feelings so immediately that Petra could only look softly at him.

'And,' Rashid continued huskily, 'I hoped—especially after the way you had given yourself to me with such wonderful passion and completeness—that you loved me. But I knew that time was running out for me, that as Rashid I could not continue to be "away on business" for much longer. And then came the desert.'

'When you couldn't take your eyes off the belly dancer!' Petra reminded him challengingly.

'I know her—after all, she is an employee of the hotel complex and she knew who I was! I was afraid that she might inadvertently give me away! But then you came to me…to my bed…and I knew I had to take a chance and find some way of keeping you permanently in my life. When you came to the hotel suite, to confront me, I seized on the opportunity it gave me to insist that we marry out of desperation.'

'But you said nothing, Rashid… You were so cold—so indifferent…'

'I felt guilty,' he admitted. 'I had railroaded you into marriage to get what I wanted…and I knew that I shouldn't have done that.'

'There are lots of things you shouldn't have done,' Petra mock reproved him. 'Including giving me a separate suite of rooms and tormenting me by letting me think that you didn't care.'

'But now you know that I do care,' Rashid whispered softly. 'You are the oasis of my life, Petra, the cool enriching gift of water to my parched desert. You and you alone have the power to make my heart bloom and flower.'

Misty-eyed, Petra listened to him.

'I want to go home, Rashid,' she told him shakily.

'Home!' He didn't try to hide either the starkness in his voice or the tormented, anguished pain in his eyes. 'You want to leave me! Perhaps I deserve it, after what I have done, but I cannot bear to let you go, Petra. Please, just give me a chance to show you, prove to you, how much I want to make you happy, to give you love. If you are not happy here in Zuran then we can live somewhere else— anywhere else that you choose—so long as you let me live there with you!'

Immediately Petra realised that he had misunderstood her, but his reaction was all the proof she could have asked for of just how much he did love her.

'I meant I want to go home with you, to our home,' she corrected his misunderstanding. 'To our home, our room, our bed...home to you, Rashid. You are my home, and wherever you are that is where my home is,' she told him with quiet sincerity.

As he wrapped her in his arms and proceeded to kiss her with fierce passion Petra could feel the fine tremble of his body.

'You know that I shall never, ever let you go now, don't you?' Rashid whispered to her. 'You are mine, Petra. My wife, my love, my life, my heart!'

The world's bestselling romance series.

HARLEQUIN®
Presents

Seduction and Passion Guaranteed!

Back by popular demand...

EXPECTING

She's sexy, successful and PREGNANT!

Relax and enjoy our fabulous series about couples whose passion results in pregnancies...sometimes unexpected! Of course, the birth of a baby is always a joyful event, and we can guarantee that our characters will become besotted moms and dads—but what happened in those nine months before?

Share the surprises, emotions, drama and suspense as our parents-to-be come to terms with the prospect of bringing a new life into the world. All will discover that the business of making babies brings with it the most special love of all....

Our next arrival will be

PREGNANCY OF CONVENIENCE
by Sandra Field
On sale June, #2329

Pick up a Harlequin Presents® novel and you will enter a world of spine-tingling passion and provocative, tantalizing romance!

Available wherever Harlequin books are sold.

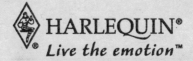

HARLEQUIN®
Live the emotion™

Visit us at www.eHarlequin.com

HPEXPJA

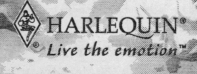

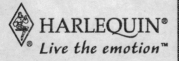

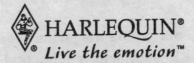

The world's bestselling romance series.

HARLEQUIN®
Presents

Seduction and Passion Guaranteed!

Coming soon...
To the rescue...armed with a ring!

Marriage is their mission!

Look out for more stories of
Modern-Day Knights...

Coming next month:
NATHAN'S CHILD
by Anne McAllister
#2333
Coming in August
**AT THE SPANIARD'S
PLEASURE**
by Jacqueline Baird
#2337

**Pick up a Harlequin
Presents® novel and
you will enter a world
of spine-tingling
passion and provocative,
tantalizing romance!**

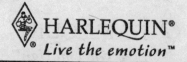

Available wherever Harlequin books are sold.

HARLEQUIN®
Live the emotion™

Visit us at www.eHarlequin.com

HPMDNNC

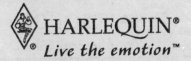